Praise for
ELIN HILDERBRAND'S

Winter Stroll

"A slice of holiday life from a master of domestic fiction....
This short, addictively readable novel is the perfect size to
squeeze in during the holiday rush."
—Susan Maguire, *Booklist*

"Hilderbrand delves deeper into the emotional lives of the
Quinn clan....Only Nantucket itself is left unscathed by the
juicy drama." —*Kirkus Reviews*

"Hilderbrand juggles an ensemble cast and successfully
weaves together many bittersweet story threads, tying up
just enough of them to keep readers anticipating another
sequel." —Kathleen Gerard, *Shelf Awareness*

"Hilderbrand ultimately triumphs in showcasing the redemp-
tive powers of forgiveness and the complex-yet-charitable
nature of family....Readers will be left anxiously anticipating
next year's conclusion to this engrossing saga."
—John Valeri, *Hartford Books Examiner*

ALSO BY ELIN HILDERBRAND

WINTER STROLL

A NOVEL

Elin Hilderbrand

Little, Brown and Company

New York Boston London

Copyright © 2015 by Elin Hilderbrand
Excerpt from *Winter Storms* copyright © 2016 by Elin Hilderbrand.

Little, Brown and Company
Hachette Book Group
1290 Avenue of the Americas
New York, NY 10104
littlebrown.com

Little, Brown and Company is a division of Hachette Book Group, Inc. The Little, Brown and Company name and logo is a trademark of Hachette Book Group, Inc.

The publisher is not responsible for websites (or their content) that are not owned by the publisher.

Printed in the United States of America

Originally published in hardcover by Little, Brown and Company, October 2015
First Back Bay paperback edition, October 2016
First Little, Brown and Company mass market edition, September 2017

10 9 8 7 6 5 4 3 2 1

*This novel is dedicated to the memory of
Grace Caroline Carballo MacEachern
(March 10, 2006–December 5, 2014)*

*and her parents, my dear and darling friends,
Matthew and Evelyn MacEachern.*

Love conquers all.

FRIDAY, DECEMBER 4

MITZI

She sneaks out behind the hotel and lights a cigarette. George knows she smokes, but he has drawn the line at watching her do it—so she has to be stealthy and quick. If she's gone for more than ten minutes he sends out a search party, which is usually comprised of himself and his Jack Russell terrier, Rudy, but also sometimes one or more of the women who work in the shop making hats. George thinks Mitzi is going to hurt herself. Or, possibly, run off and have an affair on him, the way she did on her husband, Kelley.

An affair is unthinkable in Mitzi's condition. Hurting herself seems redundant; she is already suffering from the maximum amount of pain a person can experience.

Bart Bart Bart Bart Bart.

George says he understands, but he's never had a child, so how could he possibly?

Nicotine is poison. And yet, since Bart has gone missing, cigarettes are one of two things that make Mitzi feel better. The other is alcohol. Mitzi has become partial to a sipping tequila called Casa Dragones that is packaged in a slender, elegant turquoise box and costs eighty-five dollars a bottle at the one high-end liquor store in Lenox that sells it.

She wonders if any of the liquor stores on Nantucket sell

Casa Dragones. Murray's, perhaps? She would like a few shots of it now, just enough to take the edge off.

When Bart enlisted in the Marines eighteen months earlier, Mitzi had naively believed the so-called War Against Terror to be *over.* Osama bin Laden had been killed and buried at sea. Mitzi had pictured Bart going to Afghanistan to help a war-torn people get back on their feet. She had thought he would be digging wells and rebuilding schools. She had envisioned him working with children—giving them pencils and gum, teaching them inappropriate phrases in English. *Baby got back!* But Bart had been in country less than twenty-four hours when his convoy of forty-five troops was captured.

They have been missing for nearly a year now.

The Department of Defense believes that the extremist group responsible for the kidnapping is called the *Bely,* pronounced "belle-aye." It means "yes" in the Afghan language. No one has ever heard of the Bely; all that is known about them is that they are young—most of them only teenagers— and they are vicious. One official reportedly said, "These kids make ISIS and the Taliban look like Up with People." The Bely are also, apparently, magicians—because even after sending three reconnaissance missions into Sangin and the surrounding province, the U.S. military has yet to discover where the marines are being held.

Mitzi can't watch TV anymore, nor read the newspaper; she can barely log on to her computer. When there is *definitive news* about what has happened to Bart's convoy, the DoD will contact Kelley and Mitzi directly.

George's advice is: *Try not to think about it.* This is apparently how they deal with misfortune at the North Pole. They ignore it.

Mitzi finishes her cigarette, stubs it out on the sole of her clog, and pops a breath mint—for what reason, she's not quite sure. George doesn't kiss her anymore, and they rarely have sex. George is older and requires the help of a pill to be intimate, and Mitzi can't lose herself for even half an hour. She is a prisoner as well—to her worry, her fear, her anxiety, and her bad habits.

She pulls out her cell phone and calls Kelley.

"Hello?" he says. His voice sounds robust, nearly happy; in the background, Mitzi can hear Christmas music, "Carol of the Bells." Mitzi has many issues with Kelley, but chief among them is how, at times, he doesn't even seem to remember that their son is missing. He has handled Bart's disappearance with an equanimity Mitzi finds baffling. Case in point: right now, he seems to be listening to carols! And he's probably getting ready to make champagne cocktails for the guests. It's Christmas Stroll weekend—which, on Nantucket, is even more Christmassy than Christmas itself. The town has an intoxicating smell of evergreen, salt air, and woodsmoke. When the ferry rounded Brant Point earlier that afternoon and Mitzi saw the giant lit wreath hanging on the lighthouse, she remembered, for an instant, just how much she loved the holidays on this island.

But then, reality descended like a dark hood.

"Kelley," Mitzi says. "I'm here."

"Here?" Kelley says.

"On Nantucket," she says. "For the weekend. We're staying at the Castle."

"For the love of all Harry, Mitzi," Kelley says. "Why?"

Why? Why? Why? She and Kelley had agreed that it would be best for everyone if Mitzi stayed with George in Lenox through the holidays.

"You made your decision," Kelley had said, on the other occasions when Mitzi had mentioned returning to Nantucket for a visit. "You chose George."

I chose George, Mitzi thought. For twelve years running, Mitzi and George had conducted a love affair during the Christmas holidays, when George brought his antique fire engine to the island and dressed up as the Winter Street Inn Santa Claus. Last year, things had come to a head, and Mitzi had decided to leave Kelley for George. Bart had *just* deployed and Mitzi's judgment had been wobbly. More than anything, she had wanted to escape her circumstances; she had wanted to hide in a fantasy life of sleigh bells and elves.

It had been a big fat mistake. Now that Mitzi is with George day in, day out, the allure has worn thin. Who wants to be with Santa Claus on St. Patrick's Day, or the Fourth of July? Nobody. Santa's sex appeal is specific to the month of December. On good days, Mitzi feels a brotherly affection for George; on bad days, she is filled with bitter regret.

"I had to come," Mitzi says. "I missed the island so much, and I know Kevin and Isabelle are having the baby baptized on Sunday."

"How?" Kelley says. "How did you know that?"

Mitzi crunches her breath mint. She doesn't want to give away her source.

"Ava certainly didn't tell you," Kelley says. "And it wasn't Kevin or Isabelle. And Patrick is in jail."

Another second and he'll figure it out, Mitzi thinks.

"Jennifer!" Kelley says. "Jennifer told you. I can't believe she still speaks to you. She actually *is* the nicest person alive, just as we always suspected."

"Jennifer and I are simpatico," Mitzi says. "She lost her husband, and I lost my son."

"She did not *lose* her husband," Kelley says. "Patrick is in jail, he's not *dead*. And"—here, Kelley clears his throat—"Bart isn't dead, either, Mitzi."

Mitzi squeezes her eyes shut. She can't explain how badly

she needs to hear Kelley say that. *Bart isn't dead.* Which means, Bart is alive. He's somewhere. The Bely are a new enemy, but the one thing that is known about them is their tender age. The only way Mitzi gets through some nights is to imagine Bart and the other marines playing soccer or gin rummy with their counterparts in the Bely.

When Mitzi shared this vision with George, he gave her an encouraging pat and said, "That's the ticket, Mrs. Claus."

Mitzi has become pen pals with the mothers of two of the other missing marines through a service provided by the Department of Defense, and although they are from vastly different backgrounds—one woman is a fundamentalist Christian in Tallahassee, Florida, and one woman lives on Flatbush Avenue in Brooklyn, both women are black—the emails sustain Mitzi and provide her with a sense of community. There are at least two other people in the world who understand exactly what Mitzi is feeling.

"Can I come to the baptism?" Mitzi asks. "Please?"

There is a great big huff from Kelley. "I really want to tell you 'no,'" he says. "You left *me,* you cheated on *me,* you betrayed *me,* you broke *my* heart, Mitzi."

"I know," she says. "I'm sorry."

"If it was just the one time, I might have understood," Kelley says. "But twelve years? It was a willful, planned, long-standing deceit, Mitzi."

"I know," Mitzi says. They have been over this same ground dozens and dozens of times in the past year, and Mitzi finds the best strategy is to agree with Kelley rather than try to defend herself.

"'Peace on earth, good will toward men,' Luke chapter 2, the Annunciation to the shepherds," Kelley says. "Because that is my Christmas mantra this year, I'm going to concede.

You can come to the baptism. It's at eleven o'clock on Sunday. I'll save two seats in our pew for you and George."

"Thank you," Mitzi says. She would have gone to the baptism even without Kelley's permission, but it feels better to have asked. And two seats in the family pew is more than she dreamed of.

"You're welcome," Kelley says. "Forget what I said about Jennifer. *I'm* the nicest person alive."

Mitzi hangs up the phone just as George steps out the back door of the hotel.

"I've been looking all over for you," he says. He waves two tickets in the air. "Are you ready for the Holiday House Tour?"

Bart Bart Bart Bart Bart. Mitzi always says his name five times in her mind, like a prayer.

One of Mitzi's pen pals, Gayle from Tallahassee, draws on God's strength in order to go about her normal day. Gayle works in a pediatrician's office and dealing with sick children and their parents helps keep her from dwelling on her son, KJ. Mitzi's other pen pal, Yasmin of Flatbush Avenue, stays in bed most days. She admits that she just can't return to business as usual. She quit her job as a security guard at the Barclays Center. She has a hard time doing anything but watch *Dance Moms* on TV.

Mitzi falls somewhere in between these two women. When she hears George say, *Holiday House Tour,* a part of her thinks, *Ooooooh, how Christmassy!* She had always wanted to go on the Holiday House Tour, but she'd never been able to get away from the inn on the Friday of Christmas Stroll weekend. Now that she has no inn and no guests, she can finally go. But then, the other part of her thinks, *Holiday House Tour?* How can she admire other people's festively decorated homes—the greenery, the candlelight, the precious family heirlooms—when Bart is missing?

Peace on earth, good will toward men. She will go on the Holiday House Tour. But first, for the love of all Harry, she will make George find that tequila.

AVA

Scott Skyler has done it! He has found the ugliest Christmas sweater in all the world.

He shows it to Ava in his office, after all the children and most of the staff have left school for the day. He makes her close her eyes as he puts it on. And then, she can tell, he turns off the lights in his office. Scott and Ava have been hot and heavy all year, but one thing they have not dared to do is have sex in the school. They kissed on the bench of Ava's piano back in the spring, which almost led to . . . but they stopped themselves. They climbed up to the school roof together in the middle of summer to gaze at the stars, and they almost . . . but they stopped themselves.

"Okay," Scott says. "You can open them."

Ava screams—half in horror, half in delight. It's a red wool sweater with a poufy white tulle Christmas tree on the front, decorated with actual lights that blink and flash. Ava starts to cackle. The sweater is only made better by Scott's deadpan expression; it requires someone as big and authoritative as Scott to properly pull it off.

Nathaniel would have looked ridiculous in that sweater, Ava thinks. And furthermore, he wouldn't have been a good enough sport to wear it.

It's a year later, and she *still* thinks about Nathaniel. He moved to Martha's Vineyard in the spring to build a house on Chappaquiddick for some spectacularly rich folks, and on clear days Ava squints at the horizon and wonders what he's doing over there—if he likes it better than he likes Nantucket, if he's met the Martha's Vineyard equivalent of Ava Quinn, and if he's ever coming back.

She kisses Scott. He is simply the best, truest, most excellent guy for agreeing to help her plan the Ugly Christmas Sweater Caroling party for that evening. Ava's sweater is yellow, with an embroidered picture of Jesus on the front. Jesus's hands are raised over his head. The front of his white tunic says *BIRTHDAY BOY.* Ava was proud of her sweater... until she saw Scott's sweater.

At seven o'clock on Friday night, Ava and Scott and their fellow caroling comrades gather out in front of Our Island Home, Nantucket's assisted living facility for elders. Ava's best friend Shelby, the school librarian—who is now roundly pregnant with her first child—is there, as is one of the high school English teachers named Roxanne Oliveria.

Roxanne has either forgotten or ignored the fact that this is an Ugly Christmas Sweater Caroling party, because she is wearing a rather fetching red mohair wrap sweater that shows off her fake breasts. *Hmmmmm, Roxanne,* Ava thinks. Roxanne Oliveria, called "Mz. O" by her students— the *O* salaciously drawn out to indicate "orgasm"—is of Italian descent with gorgeous thick dark hair, olive skin, and a Sophia Loren beauty mark.

Despite working two schools over, Ava has heard her fair share of gossip about Mz. Ohhhhhh. Mz. Ohhhhhh suffered through two broken engagements and as such has ended up unmarried at forty years old. She's known as a "cougar" among the kids; she prefers younger men. She dated the athletic director at the Nantucket Boys & Girls Club who was only twenty-seven at the time, and she is vaguely inappropriate with the seniors on the football team.

Ava pulls Scott aside. "How did Roxanne get invited to this?"

"I asked her," Scott says. He takes note of Ava's expression and quickly starts explaining. "I bumped into her in the hall outside the pool, and it just sort of popped out of me before I realized what I was saying."

"Does she swim laps, too?" Ava asks.

"Um...yes?" Scott says.

Swimming laps is Scott's preferred method for staying in shape. He was a backstroker at the University of Indiana, and still holds two relay titles there, a little-known fact that Ava loves about him. But now she imagines Scott swimming laps one lane over from Roxanne "Mz. Ohhhhhh" Oliveria. Does Scott admire her stroke, or her flip turns, or her fake breasts in her tank suit?

Ava takes a deep breath and thinks, *Fa-la-la-la-la, la-la-la-la.* As she discovered in her relationship with Nathaniel, Ava has jealousy issues. But she will not succumb to jealousy now and ruin their fun party. She will not.

She smiles brightly at Roxanne and hands her a songbook. "Here you go!"

"Oh, I won't be needing that," Roxanne says. "I don't sing. Scott just invited me along to be the eye candy."

The eye candy? Ava thinks. She snatches back her songbook, eighteen of which she painstakingly printed out on the school computer, and then stapled to red construction paper covers and decorated with gold glitter lettering.

She goes back to Scott and pokes him in the middle of his tulle Christmas tree. It looks like he swallowed a tiny ballerina. "Roxanne tells me you invited her along to be the *eye candy!*"

Scott laughs nervously. "Your brother is here," he says.

Saved by the bell. But Ava will not forget. She will be watching Roxanne.

"Hey, sis," Kevin says. He gives Ava a squeeze. "I'm ready to get down and *carol*." Brilliantly, Kevin has shown up in one of Mitzi's old sweaters, salvaged from a box in the attic. It's so old, Mitzi didn't even bother taking it with her when she left with George the Santa Claus. The sweater features embroidered dancing reindeer with candy-cane-striped top hats. It barely fits over Kevin's chest, it ends mid-abdomen and at his elbows.

Kevin is followed by their sister-in-law, Jennifer, who is wearing a blue mohair sweater with an elf on the front. It says: *Take me Gnome Tonight*. Jennifer is on Nantucket for the weekend with her and Patrick's three boys, who are presently at home playing age-inappropriate video games. Jennifer was a good sport to come, considering Patrick is serving jail time for insider trading at a minimum-security facility in Shirley, and he won't be released until June. But Jennifer is all about family, and there is no way she would miss the baptism. Some women, Ava realizes, would crumple in a pile and feel sorry for themselves, but not Jennifer. Jennifer puts on her gnome sweater.

Ava grabs Jennifer. "Public enemy number one tonight is Roxanne, with the boobs."

"Roger," Jennifer says.

Jennifer is the best kind of sister-in-law. She is a competitor, and when it comes down to woman-against-woman warfare, she is always in Ava's foxhole with a grenade, ready to pull the pin.

"Point her out," Jennifer says. "Nope, never mind. I see her."

They are joined by other teachers and aides from the school until they are nineteen people in all. Ava is short one caroling book, and so she decides to share with Scott.

Ava, being the music teacher, hums the key for each song.

God Rest Ye Merry, Gentlemen.
The Holly and the Ivy.
Chestnuts Roasting.

The Ugly Sweater carolers wander the corridors of Our Island Home, singing, smiling, and waving at the infirm and the bedridden until they reach the common room where a small group of residents has gathered. Some of these elders clap and sing along, and one particularly spry couple, Bessie and Phil Clay, get up to dance. Then, suddenly, Roxanne Oliveria *cuts in* on the dance. Ava is scandalized at first, but she can soon tell that Phil loves it, and so does Bessie, who collapses in her wheelchair while Phil takes Roxanne for a few spins.

Sleigh Ride.
O Come, All Ye Faithful.

And then—sigh—"Jingle Bells." Ava likes it even less this year than she did last year, but a Christmas without "Jingle Bells" is like a Halloween without jack-o'-lanterns, Valentine's Day without roses—and so on. Ava has even provided each caroler with a cluster of tiny bells to shake at the appropriate times. "Jingle Bells" is the one song Roxanne belts out, albeit off-key. The residents are eating it up, singing along themselves. No matter how old one gets, one never forgets the words to "Jingle Bells."

The residents of Our Island Home clap wildly for the carolers, and Ava leads everyone in a bow. Scott shakes hands with a few of their favorite residents. He volunteers here at Our Island Home every week, and now Ava plays the piano while he serves dinner on Friday nights. Ava has grown to love coming in; she even bought a Cole Porter songbook. Many of these older people feel sad, lonely, or neglected—and music, nearly more than anything else, reinvigorates them.

Roxanne was *kind* to dance with Phil Clay, Ava realizes. Roxanne is in the holiday spirit.

They climb into cars to head into town. Ava makes *darn* sure Roxanne isn't riding with them. Instead, Roxanne goes with Shelby and her husband, Zack, and Zack's friend Elliott, who plays the saxophone in a Bruce Springsteen cover band. Elliott would be a good match for Roxanne—what woman wouldn't love an incarnation of Clarence Clemons?—but he's too old. He's nearly fifty.

Ava and Scott are riding with Kevin, who "isn't drinking" so that he can be put on midnight duty with the baby, Genevieve. But then, he passes Ava a flask, and she takes a slug: Jameson. Of course.

Her family!

Ava says, "Are you excited about the baptism?"

He says, "Well, I wish Patrick and Bart could be here, obviously. It's a little weird being the only man left standing."

"Dad," Ava says.

"Yeah, but Dad doesn't look good lately. Have you noticed?"

"He's had a crappy year," Ava says. "His wife left him, and he nearly lost the inn. There was no way it felt good to have Mom roll in and save it."

"She really did save it, though," Kevin says. "We've been full all year. With a wait list!" Kevin has taken over the day-to-day operations of the inn, and Isabelle manages the housekeeping and cooking, and because they're both under the same roof, they can split time with Genevieve. "And it wasn't just the money."

"I know," Ava says. "But the money didn't hurt."

Margaret Quinn injected a million dollars into the inn, like adrenaline into a failing heart. But she also books a room for herself at the inn the first weekend of every month. During those weekends, she makes herself available to the guests. She hangs out in the kitchen, she helps Isabelle make the Reuben eggs Benedict, she pours coffee and draws routes in black Sharpie on the bike maps. And occasionally she holds forth on Kofi Annan, Pope Francis, Raúl Castro. The hotel guests never want to leave. They Facebook their pictures and Tweet and Instagram about the Winter Street Inn.

Margaret Quinn drew on my map! #familyheirloom #nantucket #winterstreetinn

Kelley was grateful for Margaret's help, he was very vocal about that, but neither Ava nor Kevin could figure out exactly what was going on with their parents. Margaret had her own room—room 10, George's old room, reserved especially for her—but Ava and Kevin knew that something had gone on between their parents the Christmas before. Over the course of the past year, there have been moments when they've seemed to be more than just friends. In July, they went for a long bike ride and came home completely drenched because they'd ended up at the beach and decided to swim in their clothes.

But some weekends, Dr. Drake Carroll, the pediatric brain surgeon, comes to stay with Margaret. Drake has been a handful of times, and he stays in room 10 with Margaret and they act like a couple in love. One rainy October day, they didn't emerge from their room even once. And how does Kelley feel about *that?*

Ava asked her father, "Does it bother you when Drake shows up?"

Kelley shrugged. "Drake is a great guy. And he's sending

a lot of guests our way—his patients, other doctors. I can't complain about Drake."

Ava gave him a skeptical look and Kelley said, "It's a situation that requires a lot of maturity. Thankfully, your mother and I know how to act like adults."

Scott parks on Main Street and Shelby's husband, Zack, pulls up alongside him. Nantucket is all decked out for the holidays. Along either side of the cobblestone street are brightly lit trees, each decorated by a class at the elementary school. And at the top of Main Street stands the big tree, dressed in nearly two thousand white lights. The lighting of the trees takes place the Friday after Thanksgiving, when the entire island, it seems, gathers on the cobblestones, waiting for the instant when all of the trees light up at once, a real *ahhhh* moment that captures the wonder of the season. This year, Ava and Scott took the baby, Genevieve, to the tree lighting. Scott carried Genevieve in the BabyBjörn, and he and Ava held hands and people who didn't know them thought the baby was theirs, which had given Ava unexpected pleasure. Later that night, when they had returned Genevieve to the waiting arms of her parents, Ava had said to Scott, "Can you see us having a family?"

Scott had said, "I dream of it every day."

The shopwindows are all lit up, and decorated with snowmen and candy canes, antique toys and working train sets. Ava inhales a big breath of cool air and gets a whiff of evergreen. She loves nothing more than Christmas on Nantucket. She believes in the magic.

"Scott!" Roxanne yells. She teeters over the cobblestones in her high-heeled white leather boots topped with snowy white fur. "I can't walk in these shoes. You're going to have to help me."

Ava rolls her eyes. She can't believe Roxanne is so obviously pursuing Scott's attention when she *knows* Ava and Scott are a couple. But Scott, ever the gentleman and constitutionally unable to turn down anyone in need, no matter how ludicrous that need may be, offers Roxanne one arm, and Ava his other arm, and the three of them pick their way over the cobblestones to the brick sidewalk.

Ava is relieved to reach the bar at the Boarding House, which is warm, cozy, and filled with convivial chatter. Ava is *very* ready for a drink, but they have all agreed that they will sing two songs before they order.

Ava scours her songbook for short carols. But Barry, the groundskeeper of the high school fields, who has an impressive baritone, suggests "Rudolph."

Ugh! Ava thinks. She is a classicist and considers "Rudolph" a complete abomination. However, she can't deny that it's a crowd pleaser. While they're doing songs Ava truly loathes, she figures they might as well segue into "Winter Wonderland."

The assembled crowd applauds, and there is a sharp wolf whistle that comes from the far right corner. The hair on the back of Ava's neck stands up. She knows that whistle.

She looks over. Nathaniel is sitting alone at the bar with a bottle of Whales Tale ale in front of him. He waves.

KELLEY

Kelley has heard from thousands of people offering their positive thoughts, prayers, and healing energy in regard to Bart. He has received emails from his old friends in Perrysburg,

Ohio, from guests of the Winter Street Inn whom he hasn't seen in over a decade, and from guys who worked on the commodities desk with him at J.P. Morgan in New York a lifetime earlier.

What can we do to help?

The answer: *Nothing.*

Pray.

Don't use Bart's disappearance as a springboard to air your personal views about Al Qaeda, the Taliban, or ISIS, or to disparage either the Bush administration or the Obama administration.

Don't generalize about Arab countries or Muslims.

Pray.

Nothing.

Nothing isn't quite accurate in Margaret's case. She, alone among the people Kelley knows, has offered practical action. As the anchor of the CBS *Evening News,* she is one of the most influential people in America, and has a direct line to everyone—including the president of the United States. The Oval Office assured Margaret that "every possible step" was being taken to find the missing soldiers. Margaret also has a press contact in Afghanistan named Neville Grey, who first turned up the information about the Bely, whom no one in America had ever heard of.

When Margaret asked Neville for his gut feeling on the missing convoy, Neville responded: *Most likely Bely. They're an unknown quantity. All anyone here knows is that they're kids who have been ripped from their families and trained in a culture of extreme brutality. The DoD has sent three recon missions into the surrounding region that turned up nothing. It's like these kids vanished off the face of the earth. The vehicle was unharmed, the fuel siphoned, all rucksacks and supplies taken. This kind of kidnapping is highly unusual—*

why not just blow them sky-high with an IED? My gut is that the troops are alive, and being held somewhere to be used as bargaining chips later. The Pentagon will get to the bottom of this. You just don't lose forty-five marines.

Margaret shared this with Kelley. But not knowing for sure is like living in purgatory—it's hell but not quite as bad as actual hell because there is still hope.

Hope.

In response to everyone's queries, Kelley decides, on the Friday afternoon of Stroll weekend, to compose a letter he will send out in lieu of the usual Winter Street Inn Christmas card. The card—which in years past has featured a collage of happy inn-related photos taken over the course of the year—would be inappropriate. A letter is a better idea. Kelley's mother, Frances Quinn, used to write a letter and include it with the cards she sent each Christmas—a practice that, quite frankly, Kelley found mortifying. In present-day terms, Frances Quinn might have been described as having *no filter.* In her own words, she was an Irish-American matriarch "telling it like it is," and "speaking from the heart." Frances had her predilections and prejudices and made them known in this letter, the most glaring of which was her favoritism of Kelley's brother, Avery. Every year in the Christmas letter, Avery got the first paragraph (even though he was younger than Kelley by eighteen months) and he received longer, more glowing praise. *Avery is a straight-A student. Avery is a starting guard on the freshman basketball team. Avery is president of the National Honor Society, bestowing pride on the family name.*

Kelley's paragraph always tended toward the negative. For example, one year, Frances wrote: *Kelley got a B-minus in biology this past term. It has been a challenge for Richard and me to see someone so talented not living up to his full potential. Kelley is often sullen and has become quite proficient at stomping up stairs and slamming bedroom doors. At least once a week, Richard and I consider putting him up for adoption, or encouraging him to become an exchange student in Timbuktu.*

Kelley can remember being outraged by this. *Adoption?* He'd said. *Timbuktu?*

Don't be sensitive, Frances said. *I was only kidding.*

Frances would never make such a joke about Avery, however. She was *so proud* of him when he announced he was gay during his senior year at Oberlin, and when he decided to move in with his boyfriend, Marcus, after graduating. *Avery and Marcus are cohabitating in a gorgeous brownstone on West Fourth Street in Greenwich Village, and they enjoy socializing on the weekends. Richard and I don't judge; we simply want Avery to be happy—although I do worry about the hours he keeps!*

Kelley and Avery had joked about Frances's annual Christmas letter even as Avery lay dying of AIDS in his gorgeous brownstone on West Fourth Street. It was the last thing they had laughed about together.

Mom loved me more, Avery said.

No question, Kelley said.

The Christmas letter, Avery said.

The Christmas letter, Kelley concurred. *I couldn't even get top billing when I got accepted to Columbia Business School because that was the same year you were nominated for a Tony.*

Tough luck, Avery said.

Kelley vows he will give all four of his children equal billing and he will go in order of age, which puts Bart last.

Dear Family and Friends,

Happy Holidays 2015! [Kelley spends a few minutes pondering the exclamation point. It feels too celebratory considering Quinn Family Circumstances, but using a period makes the sentence seem flat and pointless. Happy Holidays 2015. He decides to leave the exclamation point, for now.]

It has been a rough year for the Quinns, but I would like to start by saying thank you for all of the well-wishes and positive missives sent our way. Hearing from so many of you during this difficult time means more than you know.

For those of you who haven't heard, Mitzi and I have split after twenty-one years of marriage. [Kelley wonders if it will seem self-centered that he's starting with his own news. But it's basic information that "family and friends" need to know. Most of the emails and Facebook messages he's received are addressed to Kelley-and-Mitzi as a couple, and he feels compelled to end the misconception. They've been separated for nearly a year!] Mitzi has moved to Lenox, Massachusetts, with a man named George Umbrau, whom some of you will remember as our Winter Street Inn Santa Claus. [Kelley pauses and rereads. He'll let friends and family draw their own conclusions.] The silver lining to Mitzi's departure has been the return of Margaret Quinn to my life (yes, *the* Margaret Quinn: CBS *Evening News* anchor, my first wife, mother of my three older children). Margaret has been a frequent visitor to the Winter Street Inn this past year, and she has offered much-needed emotional and financial support. [He strikes "and financial." He feels shades of

Frances Quinn creeping in; nobody needs to know about the million dollars.] Margaret is the face and voice of our nation, but she is also a loving mother and my treasured friend.

Patrick was indicted in January of this year on charges of insider trading in his capacity as vice president of private equity for Everlast Investments. He's serving eighteen months at a minimum-security facility in Shirley, Mass., and is scheduled to be released in June. His lovely wife, Jennifer, continues to hold down the fort in his absence, running a successful interior design business and raising their three boys, Barrett, Pierce, and Jaime, ages eleven, nine, and seven, all of whom play lacrosse. Their other obsessions include their PS4 and Fantasy Football, a phenomenon I still do not understand.

Kevin became a father this year! He and his girlfriend, Isabelle, gave birth to a daughter, Genevieve Helene Quinn, on August 27th, an event that made Margaret and me very happy. Our first granddaughter! [Kelley wonders if he should delete that last bit. It was exciting to have a granddaughter after three grandsons, but he certainly doesn't want to offend Jennifer. After all, Kelley adores the boys and is thrilled at the continuity of the Quinn name. Neither does he want to offend Kevin. Kelley and Margaret would have been just as happy with a fourth grandson. But then again, a girl is exciting, especially for Margaret, who talks about things like taking Genevieve to see *The Nutcracker* and to the café on the seventh floor of Bergdorf Goodman for hot chocolate when she is older. He decides to leave it, for now.] Kevin and Isabelle have been instrumental in helping me run the inn now that

Mitzi has sought greener pastures with George, our former Santa Claus. [Oh, how he would love to keep that line in, but he's too nice of a guy. He strikes it.] Genevieve Helene Quinn will be baptized this Sunday at Our Lady of the Island. Both Margaret and I are looking forward to this joyous occasion. [Kelley wonders if this line makes it sound like he and Margaret are a couple. He considers adding a line informing friends and family that Dr. Drake Carroll, Margaret's boyfriend, will also be attending the baptism. But that seems like extraneous information and Drake's presence is a Christmas surprise for Margaret anyway, so Kelley just leaves the line be. People can think what they want.]

Ava continues to teach music at the Nantucket Elementary School. She has a new beau, Scott Skyler, who is the assistant principal of the school. Both Margaret and I think very highly of Scott, and hope he will become a permanent part of our family. [Kelley deletes. Ava will kill him.] This year, Ava has volunteered weekly at Our Island Home, playing piano for the residents. Scott also volunteers there, serving meals to the elderly—so, as you can see, he has been a good influence on Ava! [Kelley deletes. He will revisit Ava's paragraph later.]

PFC Bartholomew James Quinn, 1st Battalion, 9th Division, deployed to Sangin, Afghanistan, on 19 December 2014. His convoy—transporting forty-five troops to base—was announced missing by the DoD on 25 December 2014. We have little additional information, despite appeals to the nation's top brass, including our commander in chief. [Kelley deletes this. Reaching out to the Oval Office was done discreetly.] Please keep our family, and especially Bart, in your prayers.

On behalf of the Quinn family and the Winter Street Inn, I wish you a safe and joyful holiday season. Peace on earth, good will toward men.

Kelley Quinn

Kelley reads the letter through again, and considers deleting the whole thing. Divorce, jail, MIA/POW: it reads like the CliffsNotes of a Dostoevsky novel.

His phone rings.

It's Mitzi. She's on Nantucket. She wants to come to the baby's baptism.

Really? Kelley thinks. He nearly says, *You are no longer a part of this family, Mitzi. Buzz off.* But then he reads the last line of his letter. *Peace on earth, good will toward men.*

He tells her she can come to the baptism. She sounds grateful, although Kelley knows she would have showed up with or without his permission. Mitzi always does what she wants.

Kelley hangs up the phone and faces his computer. He presses Send. No regrets. In the spirit of Frances Quinn's letters, this one tells it like it is. Good, bad, or indifferent, he has spoken from the heart.

MITZI

This year, the Holiday House Tour is on Lily Street, Mitzi's favorite street on the entire island. There are five houses on the tour, each marked by luminarias placed out front. Thanks to the glowing lights and the quaintness of the shingled houses, it looks like a street in a fairy tale.

Mitzi brings George's monogrammed flask to her lips. He wasn't able to find the Casa Dragones—although he valiantly called all five liquor stores—and so she's drinking Patron Anejo.

George says, "Here's the first house. Number five."

They wait in line for nearly fifteen minutes. Where have all these people come from? Where are they staying? They aren't Nantucketers; Mitzi doesn't recognize a soul, which is a relief. She doesn't want her presence here to be a big deal; she hasn't even called her best friend, Kai, out in Wauwinet. It's a bizarre feeling, coming back to a place where she lived for so many years, but no longer lives and no longer belongs. And yet, how many times did she push Bart in his stroller down this very street? Two hundred? Five hundred? It was their preferred route into town—down to number 11 and then up Snake Alley, which brought them to Academy Hill. From there, it was a short, straight shot down Quince Street to Centre Street.

Another memory intrudes...Bart was once caught smoking weed on the steps at the top of Snake Alley with his friend Michael Bello. They were fifteen years old. Kelley had wanted to send Bart to Outward Bound that summer to get him "straightened out," but Mitzi had objected. She would never have survived an entire summer with Bart away in Wyoming or Colorado.

What are you going to do when he goes to college? Kelley asked. By that point, Kelley had already raised three children with relative success, but Mitzi felt that the upbringing of the older three had been too traditional—Patrick was an overachiever, Kevin a slacker, and Ava, the youngest and only girl, the caretaker. Mitzi wanted to do things *her* way with Bart. There had been many, many heated discussions with Kelley about this, which had usually ended with Mitzi winning.

Until, of course, the end. Bart had barely graduated from

high school, despite being incredibly gifted, and he had no interest in any more school. He refused to even *apply* to college. He spent the year after graduating living at home with Mitzi, Kelley, Kevin, and Ava. He smoked a lot of dope, crashed three cars, and according to Kevin, made all of his extra cash by stealing it.

At which point, Kelley stepped in. Over Mitzi's very loud protests, Bart joined the Marines.

Mitzi drinks from the flask.

Number 5 Lily Street has a Christmas tree decorated entirely with teddy bear ornaments, and it smells of gingerbread-scented candles. Normally, both of these things would send Mitzi into paroxysms of delight, but this year it all seems so *pointless*. George is enjoying himself, though, so Mitzi tries to drum up some holiday spirit.

George points at the mantel. "Look, honey, Byers' Choice carolers, just like yours!"

Mitzi blinks. She did have quite an impressive collection of Byers' Choice carolers, but the Mitzi who used to take half a day to unpack and arrange the figurines on the sideboard of the inn is dead and gone. Mitzi left the carolers at the inn. Maybe Kelley put them out, maybe he didn't. She doesn't care.

The woman in front of George turns around. She's a pretty, freckled redhead who looks a little bit like George's ex-wife, Patti. "I love Byers' Choice carolers!" she says. "I have all four display Santas at home: the traditional Santa, the Winter Wonderland Santa, the Deck the Halls Santa, and the Jingle Bells Santa."

"Well," George says, and Mitzi knows what's coming. "I dress up as a pretty convincing Santa myself."

The redhead squeals with delight. She sounds like a thirteen-year-old girl at a One Direction concert. "You do?"

"I was Santa for twelve years at the Winter Street Inn, here on the island," George says. "And back in Lenox, I do half a dozen holiday events for the Lions Club, District 33Y. Maybe you've heard of the Lions? We hold an annual tree and wreath sale and host three pancake breakfasts, with all proceeds going to help the blind."

"Good for *you!*" the redhead says. "Sounds like you've found a calling."

George pats his prodigious midsection. "I guess you could say I'm built for it. But being Santa is just an avocation. My real career is as a milliner. I make fine hats for women."

"No *kidding!*" the redhead says. "Just this afternoon I was thinking how much I'd like a new hat! I was dreaming of something in fur. So many of the women I saw in town were wearing fur coats."

"I make the very hat you're fantasizing about," George says. "It's fashioned from quality rabbit and chinchilla. It's like something Lara in *Doctor Zhivago* might have worn."

"Yes!" the redhead exclaims. Mitzi gazes at the birch logs stacked artfully in the fireplace and rolls her eyes. "That's exactly what I'm after."

"Here, take my card," George says. "My hats are all available for purchase online. Now, I'm warning you, they're something of an investment, but each one is crafted by hand. It's something you'll treasure for the rest of your life."

The redhead beams as though George were handing her a winning lottery ticket. George asks the redhead where she's from, and at that point, Mitzi tunes out. George loves nothing more than to chat with complete strangers, and as an innkeeper Mitzi used to be skilled at the art of small talk, but it's another thing she now finds pointless. How can she possibly converse with anyone without telling him that her only child is missing-in-action somewhere in the Helmand province of Afghanistan? And yet, that's a conversation killer, as Mitzi has learned; when she says *Helmand,* people tend to hear *Hellmann's,* and think about mayonnaise. The nice cashier at the grocery store in Lenox always asks about Bart ("Any word from your boy?"), but the mean cashier once told Mitzi that he thought the war in Afghanistan was over a long time ago. When Mitzi went home and complained to George about the mean cashier, George suggested that she go out and "make some friends." He suggested she volunteer at the women's shelter, or join a gym.

He said, "What about yoga? You used to *love* yoga."

Mitzi used to love a lot of things—yoga, gardening, reading poetry in the bath, scrapbooking, collecting shells and driftwood on the beach—and anything that had to do with Christmas. She used to spend hours making her own wrapping paper, perfecting her mulled cider recipe, and hiking through the state forest to cut greens, holly branches, and bittersweet.

But not anymore.

Mitzi maneuvers herself past George and the redhead and slips into the next room, where there is an elaborate crèche set that has been hand-carved out of some yellow waxy substance.

Mitzi stands before it, temporarily awed.

"Soap," the docent says to her. "It's all carved from soap."

Mitzi looks at the kneeling camels and the shepherds and wise men and thinks: *desert, Afghanistan.*

Bart Bart Bart Bart Bart.

She heads out the back door, then through the side yard to the front of the house where she waits for George. From down the street, she hears "The Little Drummer Boy." She closes her eyes and sings quietly along, pretending that—wherever he is—Bart can hear her. *I played my best for him, ba-rumpa-bum-bum.*

George emerges from the house with the redhead a few moments later, laughing like Santa *HO-HO-HO!* When he sees Mitzi, he sobers up.

"Hello there, Mrs. Claus," he says. "I was wondering what became of you."

The redhead peels off, heading for the next house down the street. "Nice chatting with you, George," she says. "I'll give you a call about that hat."

"You do that, Mary Rose," George says. "Happy Stroll."

Mitzi drinks from the flask. Normally, drinking takes the edge off her anxiety and sadness. It makes her feel like she's floating above the earth and that nothing is quite real. But tonight, on Nantucket, her old, strange home, everything feels jagged and in-her-face painful.

"Why is she going to *call* you about the hat?" Mitzi asks. "She can just order it online."

"She was a nice woman," George says.

Mitzi shrugs. She nearly mentions the resemblance between George's new friend Mary Rose and his ex-wife, Patti, but she doesn't want a fight. She takes a deep breath of cold night air. "I know you're not going to like this," she says, "but I'm going to walk over to the inn."

"Mitzi," George says. He's agreed to come to Nantucket only as long as Mitzi behaved herself, which means no harassing Kelley or the kids at the inn.

"I need to," she says.

George has been kind and indulgent with Mitzi to a fault, she knows. But now, he shakes his head in disgust. "If you go to the inn, you're going alone," he says.

She nods once.

"Fine," he says. "I'm going to continue on the tour, maybe try to catch up with Mary Rose."

Possibly, he's trying to make Mitzi jealous, but it's one of a thousand emotions that are beyond her.

"Okay," she says. "Have fun."

AVA

Things at the Ugly Christmas Sweater Caroling party get awkward quickly.

Nathaniel Oscar is *here,* at the Boarding House. Ava is the only one who has seen him...so far. She's so stunned, she can't even bring herself to wave back at him.

She taps Scott on the shoulder. "We need to leave," she says.

"Leave?" he says. "We just got here." He accepts a glass of red wine from Jason, the bartender. Ava assumes it's for her—she needs a drink, pronto—but then Scott hands the glass off to Roxanne, who is perched on a barstool on Scott's other side.

"You got Roxanne a drink?" Ava says.

"Yours is coming," Scott says. "Calm down."

She isn't going to be petty. It doesn't matter who gets a drink first. Ava needs to talk to Jennifer, but Jennifer is several people away, deep in conversation with Shelby and Zack.

Ava feels a tap on her shoulder. *Nathaniel.* But when she turns, she sees it's Kevin.

"Sis, I'm heading out. The inn is full and Isabelle has the baby. Plus, Mom is coming in tonight."

Ava nods. Margaret was sorry to miss the Ugly Christmas Sweater Caroling party, but she broadcasts on Fridays and generally doesn't make it to the island until late Friday evening or first thing Saturday morning, depending on whether she's flying commercial or private. It's private tonight, with her friends Alison and Zimm, furriers-to-the-stars, who are sponsoring the black-tie event tomorrow night at the Whaling Museum.

"Thanks for coming," Ava says to Kevin. "I appreciate it."

He gives her a hug. "No prob. I can't wait to take this sweater off."

"Yeah," Ava says. "Me either." If she had thought strategically, she would have worn a cute, sparkly top underneath.

Kevin's eyes wander over Ava's head. "Um...Ava? I hate to be the bearer of questionable news? But Nathaniel is sitting over there in the corner."

"Yes," she says. "I'm aware."

Kevin grins and claps her on the shoulder. "Good luck with that," he says.

Ava still has no drink. Scott is at the bar, but he's listening with rapt attention to whatever Roxanne is saying, his foot propped on the bottom rung of Roxanne's stool.

Fine, she thinks.

She heads to the other side of the bar. If Scott notices her leaving, he'll think she's headed to the ladies' room. When Ava looks up, Nathaniel's eyes are locked on hers. Her sweater starts to itch. She tells herself to turn around, take Scott's hand, plant a juicy kiss on his lips, whatever it will take for Roxanne to buzz off and Nathaniel to get up and leave.

But instead, she heads straight for Nathaniel. Nothing good can come of this.

He breaks into a big smile. "Looking good, Billy Ray," he says.

It's their old joke, and she can't help herself, she smiles. "Feeling good, Louis." Then she says, "You're back."

"That I am," he says. He stands up to give her a—well, it should have been just a friendly hug, but it turns into a squeeze. Ava has always loved the way Nathaniel smells. Like wood shavings and apples.

Ava pulls away. Nathaniel sits back down and offers Ava the stool next to his, which is conveniently empty.

She says, "I can't stay. I'm with…people." She turns around to check on Scott—he's *still* talking to Roxanne and hasn't noticed Ava missing.

"You're with Scott," Nathaniel says. "You're still dating him."

"Yes," she says.

"But you're not engaged?" Nathaniel takes hold of Ava's ringless left hand. "I thought you were so desperate to be engaged."

"Not desperate," Ava says.

"I see Shelby is pregnant," Nathaniel says.

"Yes," Ava says.

"Are you jealous?" Nathaniel asks.

"Jealous?" Ava says. "Shelby is my best friend. I'm thrilled for her." Ava *had* felt a tiny pinch of something when Shelby announced she was pregnant. It wasn't jealousy so much as fear that Ava would be left behind. She desperately wanted a husband and children.

"But you're happy with Scott, right?" Nathaniel says. "Happier than you were with me?"

"It was never a contest," Ava says.

"It felt that way," Nathaniel says. "He won, I lost."

You bought me rubber boots for Christmas, Ava thought.

Although the boots weren't the problem. The problem was that Nathaniel had always taken Ava for granted. He never made her feel special. He never treasured her the way Scott does.

Ava glances back at Scott. Still enthralled with Roxanne. What could Mz. Ohhhhhh be saying that's so interesting? Ava doesn't feel like Scott's treasure presently.

Ava says, "So, how was the Vineyard?"

"It was lonely," Nathaniel says. "The house I'm building is way out on the beach on Chappy. Beautiful spot, just not a lot of people. My apartment was in Edgartown. I would eat downstairs at this place called Atria most nights. The bartenders tolerated me. I got into a lot of heated discussions about which island is better."

"Which island is better?" Ava asks.

"Nantucket," Nathaniel says. "Because you're here."

Ava doesn't want to react to this, although she's pretty sure her heart just flipped over. But no—her heart isn't in play. She's in love with Scott.

Right?

Nathaniel says, "Can I buy you a drink?"

"God no," Ava says. "I have to get back."

"Your singing was amazing," Nathaniel says. "I could hear your voice soaring over everyone else's. You know what I really miss? I miss the way you used to sing in the truck."

"Nathaniel," Ava says. "Stop."

"Can you come over tonight?" Nathaniel asks.

"No!" Ava says.

"Please?"

"No. I'm dating Scott. You know that."

"But you're not engaged?"

"No," Ava says.

"So why don't you stop by when you're finished here?"

Nathaniel asks. "We can have a glass of wine, I'll put some wood in the stove and we can catch up. All very innocent." He lowers his voice. "Have you heard anything about Bart?"

He knows just where's she's vulnerable. Bart. Her little brother, missing. Nathaniel and Bart had been great friends, whereas Scott barely knew Bart.

For a split second, Ava is tempted. Nathaniel's cottage is cozy and charming. He has a lusciously soft blanket on his leather sofa that they used to refer to as "her" blanket. Nathaniel feeds specially treated kindling into his wood-stove that glows blue and purple through the grate. He has a great collection of wine and even better jazz records. Ava can vent all the anxieties and concerns about Bart that she's been bottling up inside—because Scott, she's certain, is tired of hearing them.

Ava holds on to her wits. "Thank you for asking," she says. "But no."

"What about tomorrow?" Nathaniel says.

Ava thinks about the next day. It's Stroll weekend, they have a full inn, and tomorrow night the entire family is going to the black-tie gala at the Whaling Museum to celebrate the Festival of Trees. Sunday is Genevieve's baptism, followed by a lunch.

"I don't have time," Ava says.

Nathaniel gives her a skeptical look.

"I'm sorry," Ava says, trying to ignore how great it feels to be turning him down. "It was nice to see you, though, Nathaniel. Happy Stroll." Ava weaves her way back to the caroling party and taps Scott on the shoulder. He turns away from Roxanne and puts his arms around her.

"Finally, you saved me," he whispers in her ear. "Roxanne is tedious."

Ava rests her head against the scratchy tulle of the Christmas tree on Scott's sweater. She closes her eyes and thinks,

Nathaniel can't do anything to win me back. But then she has a memory of riding in Nathaniel's pickup truck out to Coatue on a hot August afternoon. They were both drinking cold cans of Whale's Tale Ale, bouncing over the dunes on the beach with the windows open and the radio blaring "Bohemian Rhapsody" by Queen. Ava sang along, hitting all the high notes, and Nathaniel said, "Yeah! Go get it, sister!"

Ava remembers never wanting the song, or the moment, to end.

"Can we please get out of here?" Ava says to Scott. "Go to the next place?"

"You haven't even had a drink yet," Scott says.

Whose fault is that? Ava nearly asks him.

"Please?" she says. "I really want to sing 'Joy to the World.' Let's go to Ventuno."

"Is everyone else ready?" Scott asks. But it's clear the only person he cares about is Roxanne. "Are you ready to go to Ventuno?"

Roxanne finishes her glass of red wine and sets it on the bar and beams. "I'm ready for anything!"

She is exquisitely beautiful, Ava thinks. And she's fun. On Ava's best day she isn't half as beautiful or as fun-loving as Roxanne Oliveria. No wonder Scott is so captivated.

Scott says, "Okay, let's go then." He uses his assistant principal voice to get everyone's attention. "We're headed across the street to Ventuno!"

The group gives a cheer and puts on coats, hats, and gloves. Ava checks to make sure no one has left behind his or her songbook.

Jennifer approaches. She says, "I think this is where I peel off. The boys are probably driving Kelley batty."

"Daddy's fine," Ava says. "He loves hanging out with the kids. He told me he was going to teach them to play cribbage."

"Yeah, but it's three against one. They're probably teaching *him* to play Assassin's Creed. I should save him."

"I want you to stay," Ava says. She needs to tell Jennifer about Nathaniel.

Jennifer runs a hand through her short, dark hair, and gives Ava a weary smile. "I'm beat, Ava."

Ava hugs her sister-in-law. Jennifer puts up such a strong, implacable front that it nearly masks the fact that Patrick is in jail and Jennifer has been left to handle everything in his absence. She has, essentially, become a disaster specialist and a triage nurse. She dealt with the state's attorney office and the local media blitz; she stood by Patrick publicly and privately. She has kept life as normal as possible for the boys, and she's managed to proceed with two massive interior design projects.

"Go home and get some sleep," Ava says.

"I'm stopping at Murray's for a couple bottles of chardonnay on the way home," Jennifer says. "Your mom will probably want a glass when she gets here."

"Good idea," Ava says. Kevin is normally in charge of making sure there's alcohol in stock at the inn, but since the baby was born, he has, understandably, lapsed in his duties.

Jennifer leaves the bar and Ava waits for Shelby and Zack and Scott—and Roxanne. She can't help herself from turning around one more time to look at Nathaniel.

Come over, he mouths, pointing to his watch. *Later.*

Ava smiles and shakes her head.

Ventuno is so close to the Boarding House that Ava can throw a softball at it. And yet, the second they embark on the journey, there is drama.

Roxanne falls down in the cobblestone street. She starts screaming.

Ava and Scott rush over to where Roxanne is huddled in a heap, clutching her ankle. Ava sucks in her breath. The ankle is twisted at a gruesomely unnatural angle. Broken.

Scott whips out his phone and dials 911.

Elliott the saxophonist says, "We need to get her out of the street." He looks to Zack. "Should we carry her over to that bench?"

"You're not supposed to move her," Barry the grounds-keeper says. "Leave her be until the ambulance gets here."

"I think that's only the case with head trauma," Shelby says. "I think we should get her out of the road."

Roxanne is howling with pain and Ava's skin prickles beneath her scratchy sweater. Scott is kneeling next to Roxanne, holding both of her hands in his, murmuring words of comfort. Ava shuts her eyes. That ankle does not look right; just thinking about how the doctor will have to set it makes Ava cringe. Roxanne will most likely have to have surgery, which means she will be taking the Med Flight to Boston.

The ambulance arrives with sirens blaring and lights flashing antagonistically amongst all the holiday lights. The Ugly Sweater carolers are gathered in a loose knot around Roxanne but when the paramedics hop out, they disperse.

Shelby squeezes Ava's arm. "I hope the heels were worth it."

It was, by anyone's standards, a poor choice of footwear, but Ava can't even blame Roxanne for her vanity. Roxanne shrieks as the paramedics lift her onto the stretcher. There is no way she is exaggerating for Scott or anyone else's benefit. The woman is in serious pain, and Ava thinks, *Oh please, please let her be okay.*

The paramedics load Roxanne into the back of the ambulance—and away they go to Nantucket Cottage Hospital.

Scott finds Ava in the crowd. "Bummer," he says.

"Huge," she says. The Ugly Sweater Caroling party has come to a crashing halt. There will be no Ventuno, no Town, no Dune, no last call at Lola, and no "Joy to the World."

Ava says, "Should we go to the hospital?"

Scott says, "I'll go and make sure she gets admitted. You don't have to come."

"I feel responsible," Ava says. "This was my party. If I hadn't organized it, Roxanne wouldn't have broken her ankle."

"*I* feel responsible," Scott says. "I'm the one who invited her. And I was going to offer to help her cross the street, but I thought you'd get angry."

"So that makes it doubly my fault," Ava says.

"It was Roxanne's fault for wearing those silly heels," Scott says. "She couldn't walk in them sober, never mind with a glass of wine and a shot of Jameson in her."

"Shot of Jameson?" Ava says.

"Kevin offered her the flask," Scott says. "While you were in the bathroom."

While Ava was in the bathroom.

"I'll come with you to the hospital," Ava says.

"You don't have to," Scott says. "Really. You have a big weekend and your mom is coming tonight. You should go home. I'll text you and let you know what the doctors say."

"But—"

"Ava," he says. He holds her chin in that way he has, and he kisses her. "I'll text you." He swats her butt before he starts walking down the street toward his car. Ava realizes then that he doesn't *want* her to come, not even to keep him company. He wants to be the hero for Roxanne alone. Or, possibly, because he's an administrator and Roxanne is a teacher he feels he must go and serve as a lieutenant to one of his troops. Or, he is really, truly thinking of Ava. *Does* she want to spend the next three hours sitting in the emergency room? No.

However, Scott has left her without a ride home. Has he even considered this? True, Winter Street is only at the top of Main, but it's pretty cold out for that kind of walk. Ava will have to get a ride from Shelby and Zack, but when she looks around, they're gone.

Ava pops back into the Boarding House to see if they've gone inside to warm up but Ava doesn't see them. Shelby gets tired easily, and she's not drinking; Ava bets they've headed home.

Ava's eyes dart to the corner of the bar. Nathaniel's seat is empty.

He left.

Ava's heart drops an inch. It might have been nice to have talked with him without Scott *right there*. She could have told him what little she knows about Bart.

Ava considers having a drink by herself, a hot toddy, something to combat the frigidness of her impending walk home, but she's the elementary school music teacher and thus has a certain image to uphold, plus she doesn't want to grow reflective about Nathaniel, or maudlin about Bart.

She bundles up and heads back outside. She makes it as far as the corner of India and Main Street when a truck pulls up alongside of her.

Nathaniel's truck. The passenger window goes down and Nathaniel says, "Need a ride?"

Actually," Ava says, "I do." And without giving it another thought, she hops in.

KELLEY

He knows Jennifer has been having a hard time with Barrett, the oldest of the Quinn grandchildren, who is the spitting image of Patrick and in many ways, the spitting image of Kelley himself. Part of what Jennifer is dealing with is regular eleven-year-old-boy sullenness, but on top of that, the kid's father is in jail. Barrett is angry, he's embarrassed, humiliated, ashamed, and he wants to know why he has to follow the rules if his father didn't.

Once Jennifer leaves for the caroling party, Kelley decides to have a man-to-man chat with Barrett, and Pierce could probably stand a little grandfather lecture as well.

Kelley has to be quick with the remote—which he is—and firm. TV off.

"Grandpa!" Pierce says.

"I need to talk to you and you," he says, pointing to the two elders.

"What about me?" Jaime says.

Jaime is seven which is a little young for the things Kelley wants to say. "You should go down to the kitchen and ask Isabelle if there are cookies."

"Okay," Jaime says.

"Bring me some," Pierce says.

"Can't this wait?" Barrett asks Kelley.

"It cannot," Kelley says.

The boys reluctantly drop their controllers and sink back into the sofa. If Kelley had been thinking, he would have brought up a bribe—root beer floats, or Starbursts. Or are Barrett and Pierce too old to be placated with sweets? Kelley's own grandfather had a farm with horses and a pond stocked with trout. Pops was a top-notch grandfather; Kelley can only hope to measure up.

"You two have to take it easy on your mother," Kelley says.

"I do take it easy on her," Pierce says.

Barrett is quiet.

"She's under a lot of stress," Kelley says.

"She picks wallpaper, and upholstery fabric," Barrett says. "You can't tell me that's stressful?"

"She's running a business," Kelley says.

"She yells at us to get our homework done, but she doesn't help us with it anymore. She makes us unload the dishwasher and take out the trash but half the time she forgets to give us our allowance. She tells us to *pick up the slack,* but what she doesn't seem to *get* is that we lost our father."

Kelley tents his fingers the way he remembers his own grandfather doing; it feels like a gesture of wisdom. "Your father made a mistake. It's unfortunate, but you have to remember that he isn't gone forever. He'll be back this summer, and you want him to be proud of how you acted in his absence."

"Why should we care if he's proud of *us?*" Barrett says. "We aren't proud of him. He's supposed to *lead by example.*"

"What you'll find in life," Kelley says, "is that everyone is fallible. Everyone makes mistakes. Everyone messes up. Even dads."

"I have a D in Spanish," Pierce says. He hangs his dark head. Barrett and Jaime are as redheaded and freckled as leprechauns, but Pierce has inherited his mother's black Irish beauty. "My teacher speaks only in Spanish and I can't understand her, and then I get in trouble for not following instructions."

"Idiot," Barrett says.

"Barrett," Kelley says, "I want you to *stop* with the name-calling and with the ill will toward your parents. They're human beings."

"They used to be cool," Barrett says. "Everything was fine. Then Dad messed up and Mom...honestly, she makes everything worse."

"She dropped a pot of spaghetti on the floor," Pierce says. "Then she tried to clean it up with the vacuum cleaner, then the vacuum exploded and she cried."

"Really?" Kelley says. He has a hard time picturing Jennifer in that particular scenario. Mitzi, yes; Jennifer, no.

"She's turned into a complete psycho," Barrett says.

"Barrett," Kelley says. "Enough."

Kelley tries to remember if Patrick and Kevin were ever this disrespectful. They must have been! When they were younger, and Kelley and Margaret and the kids all lived in the brownstone on East Eighty-eighth Street, there was a lot of squabbling, but Kelley let Margaret deal with the discipline while he spent fourteen-hour days worrying about the overseas markets. Once Kelley left Wall Street behind and moved to Nantucket to run the inn, he used to wake Patrick and Kevin up at the crack of dawn to do DIY projects, and then, as a reward, he would take them to the Brotherhood of Thieves for burgers. They watched college basketball together, and they had a dirty joke contest running for a while. Kelley had never crossed the line of being friends with his sons, but they had had good moments.

"Seriously, Grandpa, there's something else going on with Mom," Barrett says. "She's either all wound up, or else she's so mellow, it's like she's sleepwalking."

Is she drinking too much? Kelley wonders. And if so, can he blame her? Is she smoking *dope?* The mere thought of straitlaced Jennifer smoking a joint makes Kelley smile.

"Just remember, your mom is suffering, too. She misses your dad."

"Do you miss our dad?" Pierce asks.

"Yes," Kelley says. "Yes, I do."

"But you miss Uncle Bart more, right?" Pierce says.

"The situations are different," Kelley says. "Your dad is in Shirley, and I go visit him once a month and I know when he's coming back. Your Uncle Bart is a prisoner of war. I don't know if he's safe and I don't know when he's coming back. So I guess you might say I'm more concerned for Bart. But I miss them both a great deal."

"I like Uncle Bart," Pierce says. "I want to be in the Marines."

"They'll never take you," Barrett says. "You're too annoying."

Okay, Kelley thinks. He's done here. He tried. He switches on the TV just as Jaime walks into the room eating a chocolate chip cookie.

"Where's mine?" Barrett says.

"It was the last one," Jaime says.

Before Barrett can reach out to punch his brother, Kelley turns back to the TV.

"Go back to stealing cars," he says. "I'll make some more cookies."

The boys grab their controllers. Kelley stands in the doorway to the den for a second, watching them. He's pretty sure that his words of wisdom have had zero effect.

Pierce glances up and smiles. "Thanks, Grandpa," he says. "Good talk."

JENNIFER

The woman in front of Jennifer at Murray's Liquors looks familiar, even from the back. It's something about the angular cut of her hair, and the severe red and black dye job. Jennifer can't quite figure out who it is...not someone from Beacon Hill, she doesn't think...possibly someone from here? But how many people does Jennifer know on Nantucket? Not many.

Then the woman spins around clutching a bottle of Smirnoff vodka and a bottle of Kahlúa by the neck and Jennifer sees the snake tattoo jumping off the woman's neck. It's not a tattoo that anyone forgets. Jennifer gasps.

"Norah!" Jennifer says. "Hi!"

The woman sniffs at Jennifer and marches out of the store with her purchases.

Jennifer sets her two bottles of cold chardonnay on the counter and tries to collect her wits.

Did that just happen?

Norah Vale, Kevin's ex-wife? Here, on Nantucket? On the weekend of Genevieve's baptism? *Norah Vale,* Jennifer thinks. *Cautionary Tale.* The way Norah was holding the bottles made it seem like she was heading home to make some Black Russians. Was she *living* here? Norah Vale grew up on Nantucket. Possibly she was just home visiting her family. The family situation is a hot mess, if Jennifer remembers correctly. The mother has six children by three men, but Norah, the youngest, shares a father with the oldest brother— because, as Norah once phrased it, her mother saw nothing wrong with making the same mistake twice. The father isn't in the picture anymore, but Norah used to be close with her older brother, Danko, the tattoo artist. Danko was the genius who had talked Norah into the trompe l'oeil python that looks like it's striking from off Norah's neck.

Jennifer pays for the wine, takes the bag, and hurries up Main Street with half an idea that Norah Vale is lurking behind a tree somewhere, intending to jump out and harm Jennifer.

For six years, they were sisters-in-law, married to brothers, a delicate relationship to manage under the best of circumstances, but Norah and Jennifer had really hated each other. Which is more accurately to say that Norah had hated Jennifer while Jennifer tried to be as kind and patient and accommodating with Norah as possible, but Norah found Jennifer's attention—even the most innocuous comments— patronizing. Jennifer was, in Norah's words, a "snobby pop-tart," whatever that meant. Norah resented that Jennifer had grown up on Nob Hill in San Francisco, that she had graduated from Stanford, that she wore Ray-Ban aviators and carried Coach handbags, that she and Patrick devoted so much time and energy to "being perfect."

When Jennifer assured Norah that she was far from perfect, Norah had responded with some choice expletives.

Jennifer desperately needs to talk to Patrick. She feels the urge to call him seventy or eighty times a day, but she can't—nor can she email or text. He's only allowed one half-hour phone call per week, which is always scheduled for Sunday afternoons at four.

But by Sunday afternoon at four, the baptism will be over, and Jennifer needs him now. He's been in jail for almost an entire year, and yet it still feels surreal. Every morning for nearly a year, Jennifer has woken up—often Jaime, her youngest, has climbed in with her, an egregious habit she allows because she knows how much he misses his father— and she has thought, *My husband is in jail*.

Jail.

It has such a *stigma*, it's so beneath a person of Patrick's caliber, it indicates such nefarious behavior and bad judgment that even now, eleven months later, Jennifer can't believe it.

She didn't think she would be able to face any of her

friends or any of her and Patrick's Beacon Hill neighbors, or any of the other parents at the kids' schools. But Jennifer's best friend Megan stood stalwartly by her. Megan is a breast cancer survivor—she went through a double mastectomy, chemo, radiation, the whole bag of tricks—and because of this she is revered, and widely considered a hero. When Megan supported Jennifer, everyone else who mattered followed suit, and Jennifer enjoyed a kind of reverse celebrity. Rather than judging her or hating her, people seemed to pity her. Or maybe they didn't pity her, maybe they just understood that Patrick had made a mistake and crossed a line in his tightly regulated business. *Insider trading.* Many people referenced Martha Stewart, who had served her time for the same crime, and then bounced right back to making buttercream icing and mulching the peonies.

Megan had also given Jennifer a stash of pills: oxycodone for during the day ("It's jet fuel," Megan said) and Ativan to help her sleep. At first, Jennifer turned down the offer of the pills, but Megan insisted. ("Just take them in case you need them, Jen. I'm not suggesting you become an addict, but suffering through a crisis like this without a little pharmaceutical help is unnecessary martyrdom.") Jennifer took the pills and buried them deep in her purse. Just in case.

As it turned out, not everyone was interested in letting Jennifer off the hook. A mother of twins in Pierce's grade named Wendy Landis lobbied fiercely to have Jennifer removed from the parents association, citing the Quinn family's "poor choices and lack of integrity." Jennifer had taken this *very* hard. Wendy Landis was a member of Jennifer's church and she lived only six houses away on Beacon Street. Jennifer had always idolized Wendy Landis for having a career—she was a named partner at one of the best law firms in the city—and somehow also being one of those everything moms.

Jennifer took her first oxycodone before she went into a meeting with the headmaster of Pierce's school to combat Wendy Landis's slur campaign against her. Megan had been right: the oxy made *everything* better. It gave Jennifer wings and cast a golden glow of optimism over the entire situation. Jennifer explained to the headmaster that *she* had not committed a crime; in fact, *she* had earned an A in her Introduction to Ethics class at Stanford, and as for Patrick, he had fully admitted his wrongdoing and was now paying his debt to society.

The headmaster had sided with Jennifer; she would remain on the executive board of the parents association. Jennifer felt so vindicated when she walked out of the school that she took another oxy in celebration. Unfortunately, she felt herself slipping down the back side of that pill at the same time that the boys arrived home from school with their attendant clamor and chaos, and so she took a third pill. The third pill kept her revved-up, but with a bit of a manic edge; she engaged Barrett in yet another embittered confrontation about his bad attitude. By the time the effects of the third pill wore off, it was time for Jennifer to pour herself a glass of wine, but the wine didn't settle her like it normally did, and so Jennifer also popped an Ativan.

The combination of the wine and the Ativan was magnificent! Suddenly Jennifer could see how manageable everything was, despite Patrick's absence. She floated around the kitchen making pumpkin risotto and a kale Caesar salad, and at the end of the meal she asked the boys to clean up while she retreated to her room and fell promptly asleep.

The next morning, she woke up dry-mouthed and sluggish—and so she decided to take an oxy, just to get her day kick-started.

Does she need to explain how easy it was to fall prey to

the magic power of pills? It was easy. Megan had given her forty oxycodone—forty!—and thirty Ativan. At the time, it had seemed like enough to last the rest of Jennifer's life, but her supply steadily dwindled. Jennifer was able to have the Ativan prescribed by her own doctor "for anxiety," but Jennifer had to go back to Megan and ask for more oxycodone. Megan gave her twelve more pills without any words of judgment, but Jennifer can't go back to her friend again, and she only has seven pills left.

When they're gone, she tells herself, they're gone, and she'll have to do without.

Her pharmaceutical addiction presently tops her list of concerns. She's doing okay financially. Despite the cost of lawyers and Patrick losing his job at Everlast, there is still plenty of money in the bank to live on, for a while at least, and Jennifer's two design projects will bring in a nice six-figure salary.

Jennifer's other problem is that she's lonely. She misses Patrick's physical presence, his weight and warmth in bed at night, his keen intellect, his fire and enthusiasm, his smile, his voice, his every-second-of-every-day friendship. She misses not being free to call him or text him; it's as if she is in prison as well.

Right now, Jennifer would like to call Patrick to ask if he thinks Norah Vale has been back on Nantucket for a while, or if he thinks she just arrived. Maybe Norah got here days or weeks ago and Kevin already knows and has dealt with it. Maybe Kevin and Norah have had a détente; maybe they're friends.

But Jennifer doesn't think so. The withering look Norah gave her, and the sniff, suggested warfare.

If Kevin knew Norah was back on Nantucket, he would have told Ava and Ava would have told Jennifer. Unless they didn't want to bother Jennifer with it. Since Patrick has gone to jail, the Quinns have tried to shield Jennifer from bad news. She was the last one to hear about the terrorist group they think has captured Bart.

Jennifer calls Ava's cell phone. No answer. Ava is probably still out caroling, and Jennifer is *not* going to ruin her fun time by bringing up the poisonous topic of Norah Vale. Jennifer doesn't want Ava to worry when she sees a missed call, however, so she leaves a message.

"Hey, it's Jen. Nothing major, just wanted to ask you about something, but it can wait until morning. The caroling was fun. Thanks for including me!"

Jennifer pockets her phone and hurries up the street toward the inn with the wine. She thinks of how nice it will be to relax with a cold glass of chardonnay. And then, she will take an Ativan and go to sleep.

DRAKE

He's never done anything like this in his life. He has many admirable qualities, but spontaneity isn't one of them.

The only person who knows he's decided to come to Nantucket this weekend is Kelley, and Kelley has been more agreeable about Drake showing up than Drake expected. Drake hopes this is because Kelley has finally realized that he and Margaret do not have a romantic future. Margaret admits that she was torn for a while; she told Drake about what happened between her and Kelley last Christmas.

But it won't happen ever again, she told Drake. *I don't love him the right way and we don't want the same things.*

Drake was relieved to hear this. It took him a while to drum up the courage, but he finally said to Margaret over a romantic dinner at Eleven Madison Park: *You know what? I think we want the same things.*

Margaret had given him a skeptical look. She said, "Yes. We want to work eighteen hours a day, sleep for five and a half, take a twenty-minute shower, and have sex in the remaining ten."

Am I that bad? he wondered. He knew she was kidding, but some of her assessment felt true. For a long time, Drake had considered himself too busy for love. He was a pediatric brain surgeon at Sloan Kettering, which meant that day in, day out, he removed tumors and inserted shunts and clipped aneurysms in patients aged three months to sixteen years. He performed up to twelve surgeries a week and saw patients for consultations or follow-ups an additional twenty-five to thirty hours a week, then there was endless paperwork, his team of three residents to oversee, and he presented papers at conferences twice a year. He was also a runner—ten miles every Saturday and Sunday, and three miles on Wednesday evenings when he could squeeze it in.

He'd never been married and never had any children of his own. He loved kids; nine times out of ten, he would rather deal with a sick child than a sick child's parents. It was because of the parents that Drake had never wanted children himself. He'd been witness to way too much heartbreaking emotional pain. When he was doing his surgical residency at CHOP in Philadelphia, he'd attended on an eight-year-old patient named Christopher Rapp who had a malignant growth in the thalamus that most surgeons wouldn't have bothered trying to resect. It was too deep, and the danger of dying on the table too great, but the alternative was to let the tumor metastasize and watch near-immediate debilitation—

the kid would be blind in two months and unable to eat or speak in four. The child's father, a man named Jack Rapp, had pushed for the surgery, despite the risks. Jack Rapp was a single parent—the mother hadn't been heard from since Christopher was an infant—and Christopher was an only child. Jack Rapp was as tough a man as Drake had ever encountered. He'd been a marine in Vietnam, stationed in Da Nang for thirty-nine months, and he now owned asphalt plants that provided material for half the highways in Pennsylvania—but he was *destroyed* by Christopher's illness.

You've got to save him, man, Jack Rapp said. *He's all I've got.*

Christopher had died on the table, and Drake, pulling the short straw, had been the one to inform Jack Rapp. The man had crumpled. That was the only word for it. And then, four hours later, Jack Rapp was found dead himself in his car in the parking garage. Gunshot to the head.

Drake knows that love of one's child is the most powerful love there is, and he's always been terrified of it. Ditto romantic love, which always seemed to result in a lack of control that has no place in his life.

Until now. He recently forced himself to face the startling fact that he is *in love with Margaret Quinn*—and *not* the Margaret Quinn everyone in America watches on TV each night, with her bright smile and her soothing, melodious voice. (*Time* magazine once said that Margaret could deliver news of genocide or an assassination and make it sound like a bedtime story.) Drake is in love with the Margaret Quinn who snorts when she laughs, and who knows all her doormen by first and last name. Drake is in love with the Margaret who douses her oysters with Tabasco, then lets out a "Whoo!" after she sucks one down. He is in love with the Margaret of the soft, pale skin with freckles on the backs of her knees who reads *The Economist* to put herself to sleep.

That she has reported from sixty-two countries and has dined with the last four presidents does impress him, but it's not why he loves her. Drake loves Margaret because she is smart—possibly even smarter than the incredibly brilliant female surgeons and medical oncologists Drake works with—and she is fun, irreverent, and incredibly kind. She adores her children and her grandchildren, and her greatest wish is that she might be cloned so that she can always be in two places at once.

It is only in this past year that she's gone to Lee Kramer, the studio president, for time off so she could come to Nantucket to help Kevin and Isabelle with the baby, and lend her star power to lure more paying guests to Kelley's inn.

Margaret invited Drake to join her a handful of times, but twice in a row he had conflicts, and he feared she would stop asking.

Margaret *had* invited him this weekend, which is significant not only because it's Christmas Stroll weekend but also because the baby, Genevieve, is being baptized on Sunday. Initially, however, Drake declined. He had surgery scheduled late Friday afternoon and early Monday morning, a backlog of paperwork rivaling that of most state governments, and quite frankly, the thought of dealing with all of Margaret's family intimidated him.

Margaret accepted his excuses with her usual grace, but he could tell she was disappointed, and in the days following, he didn't hear from her at all. His calls went straight to her voicemail. Drake took it in stride the first few times, then he grew miffed. Was she *freezing him out?* She always said she realized that he had a big job and was very, very busy. Then, after four days, he started to worry. Had he just *blown it* with Margaret Quinn?

He gave his Friday surgery to his most trusted colleague

and postponed Monday's surgery; he crammed paperwork into his briefcase, he packed his tuxedo for the black-tie event Margaret had mentioned, and a pink tie for the baptism. He arrived at the Winter Street Inn at seven o'clock, and Isabelle, Kevin's lovely French fiancée, showed him to room 10.

She said, "Kelley is playing shooting games with the boys and Kevin is singing in town with Ava. You will be fine, yes or no?"

"Yes," Drake said, but he felt nervous. For one second, he wondered if Margaret had invited someone *else* to be her guest for the baptism weekend. A few years ago, she had dated Jack Nicholson. What if Margaret shows up with Jack?

Something about the inn relaxes him. It's all decked out for Christmas—with a fresh garland tied off with burgundy velvet bows, a huge glittering tree, a mantel crowded with nutcrackers. There is classical Christmas music playing, which Drake prefers over Bing Crosby. "The First Noel." The hospital had just been putting up their trees when Drake left that afternoon, but no matter how much money the Sloan Kettering fund-raising committee provides to decorate at Christmas, the hospital always feels melancholy.

Drake brings his paperwork down to the large leather sofa in the living room and, as there are no other guests around, he spreads out. He loosens his tie and kicks off his chocolate suede Gucci loafers. There's a fire crackling in the fireplace and almost immediately Isabelle brings him a double Grey Goose and tonic with lime, which is his preferred cocktail, and a plate of cheese puffs, warm from the oven.

"Merci!" Drake says. And then, because he's really been

trying to get his head out of his work and improve his interpersonal skills, he asks, "How's the baby? *L'enfant? Genevieve?*"

"Beautiful," Isabelle says, and she winks. "Sleeping."

He's not sure what time Margaret is supposed to arrive. She's flying in on her friend Alison's private plane sometime after her broadcast, which ends at seven.

She could be here as early as eight thirty, he supposes. Or far later.

Please let her be alone, he thinks. *And let her be happy to see me.*

He's halfway through his second drink and has devoured the plate of cheese puffs plus the entire dish of mixed nuts, which is meant for all the inn's guests, when the front door to the inn swings open.

Margaret! he thinks. And he stands up.

But the woman who wanders in isn't Margaret. It's a frightfully skinny woman with curly hair buttoned snugly into a forest green wool coat, with a scarf that looks like a long Christmas stocking wound around her neck.

The woman has a look in her eye that Drake recognizes only too well. It's a look he sees every day, in the eyes of mothers whose children have been diagnosed as terminal. It's a particular kind of naked, desperate pain.

"Good evening?" Drake says.

The woman gives him a genuinely quizzical look, as if he had just intruded on her quiet work space, and not the other way around. "Who are you?"

He laughs. "I'm Dr. Carroll. Who are *you?*"

She takes a flask from her pocket and upends it into her mouth. "Are you a guest of the inn, then?"

He nods. "Are you?"

"I'm looking for Kelley," she says. "Is he around?"

"Last I heard, he was playing shooting games," Drake says, then he chuckles at how that sounds. "With his grandsons, I assume, I'm not sure. I haven't seen him. I can get the manager for you. Isabelle."

"No, no," the woman says. She collapses on the sofa. "I'm not supposed to be here."

Drake regards the woman, whose eyes are now scanning his patient notes, which are, of course, extremely confidential. He gathers them up, keeping one eye on the woman, wondering if she is an itinerant off the street.

"So you're not a guest of the inn?" he says. "Are you a friend of Kelley's?"

The woman starts to cry. Drake can't help himself; he goes right into doctor mode. He has worked all these many years to uphold his professional shield, but the truth is, he's compassionate to a fault. He settles down on the sofa next to the woman and takes her hand. She squeezes with all her might, crushing his fingers. Drake has experienced this too many times to count with the mothers of his patients.

He says, "Ma'am..."

The woman sobs. She says, "You have *absolutely no idea* what it's like."

Drake hands her the damp cocktail napkin from under his drink. He thinks, *The road to hell is paved with good intentions.* He should have waited for Margaret up in room 10.

The woman blows her nose on the napkin, then rests her head against the sofa cushion and unbuttons her coat. "It looks really nice in here. I've forgotten how cozy it is by the fire."

"So you've been here before?" Drake asks.

She closes her eyes. "I'm pretty drunk," she says. "Alcohol is the only thing that helps."

The woman looks overly comfortable, like she might fall asleep. Drake should either head upstairs to the room or venture out to find some dinner. Sitting here next to a drunk stranger isn't a good idea.

The woman murmurs something he doesn't understand.

"I'm sorry?" he says.

"The nutcrackers," she says. "Which is your favorite? Mine is the astronaut."

"Oh," Drake says, grateful for a relatively safe topic of conversation. "The doctor, I think." The doctor nutcracker is old-fashioned, like something out of a Norman Rockwell painting. He's wearing a headband mirror and a stethoscope and carrying an inoculation syringe. Drake blinks and imagines himself as a nutcracker, brandishing his cranial saw and his ultrasound probes. The two vodkas are taking effect; even on a regular weekend at home, he never allows himself two double cocktails like this. He wonders if it's narcissistic to answer "the doctor" when he *is* a doctor, so he tries again.

"And I like the Oktoberfest nutcracker. I've always meant to go to Oktoberfest, but I've never had time. I guess you could say it's on my bucket list." Now he *knows* he's getting drunk. Never in his life has he used the term "bucket list." It has always seemed silly; in his daily life, his "bucket list" is to save as many children's lives as possible. However, now that he's nearly sixty with retirement a mere five years away, and now that his feelings for Margaret have escalated in such a dramatic fashion, he's starting to think of the things he'd like to do with her—sooner rather than later. The Great Barrier Reef. Cinque Terre. The Great Wall.

The woman bursts into fresh tears. "My son... back from Munich!" she says.

Drake doesn't quite catch that. What he thinks she said is

that her son just got back from Munich? "Oh," he says. "Was he doing business there? Or traveling? There used to be a thing called a Eurail pass. I wonder if that still exists?"

The woman is crying too hard to answer, and Drake finally admits to himself that he has gotten in over his head in this conversation, and he needs help. The inn is filled with guests, but there isn't a soul around; everyone must be out enjoying the charms of Christmas Stroll. Drake needs to somehow summon Isabelle, or even Kelley, but he's afraid that if he calls out, he'll wake the baby. The woman is listing precariously toward him; she's threatening, perhaps, to rest her head on his shoulder.

Drake says, "I'm sorry. I wish there was something I could do to help."

"My son!" she wails. "There is absolutely *no way* you could know how this feels."

Drake moves on his hunch. "Is he sick?" he asks.

"Is he *sick?*" the woman says, her tears clearing up a bit. She sniffles and mops her face with the soggy cocktail napkin. "I have no way of knowing if he's sick or well—that's the thing. I know *nothing,* and when a mother knows nothing, her mind goes to the darkest places."

Against his better judgment, Drake tosses back the last inch of his drink. Somewhere in the house, a clock chimes the half hour, and Drake discreetly checks his watch. Eight thirty already! He might as well sit tight until Margaret arrives and they can go to dinner together. Their favorite spot, 56 Union, is serving a special holiday menu until ten.

Drake places a hand lightly on the woman's arm. "Listen," he says. "I deal with a lot of unlucky mothers. I deal with mothers who have just discovered their five-year-old daughter has stage four brain cancer. I deal with mothers whose three-month-old infant son needs a shunt implanted to relieve the pressure in his skull, or he will die. Can you imagine how hard it is to entrust your three-month-old baby to a surgical team? Or your five-year-old little girl?"

The woman has stopped crying.

"Do you know what I tell those mothers? I tell them to have faith in the good forces of this world. I tell them to hope. I tell them to pray to whatever higher being they believe in. I tell them to trust the medical marvels of our day and age and the natural talent and excellent training of their surgeons." Drake takes off his glasses and sets them on the table so that he can better look this woman in the eye. "But mostly, I tell them to remain positive. To visualize a *positive outcome*."

The woman nods slowly and then—then, there's a trace of a smile. "Thank you," she says. "Thank you for listening. Thank you for being nice to a complete stranger. My boy-friend and my estranged husband and so many other people treat me like I'm an inmate at the asylum. There isn't any way to make me feel better, and I understand that's frustrat-ing for the people who love me. But instead of accepting my grief as real and legitimate, they write me off as crazy."

Well, the woman *is* a little crazy as far as Drake can tell. He needs to gently excuse himself and go up to his room. But he feels a small sense of accomplishment because he's managed to get her calmed down.

She looks at his paperwork as he gathers it up. "You're a doctor?" she says. "Can you write me a prescription?"

Crazy, he thinks. "Only if you're a patient," he says.

"Maybe I'll become a patient," she says. "What's your name?"

"Dr. Carroll," he says. "But you can call me Drake. What's yours?"

"Mitzi Quinn," she says, and without warning, she reaches over to embrace him.

Drake tries to back away but she's too quick—and surprisingly strong. He is caught in her hug as he processes the name *Mitzi Quinn*. His brain is swimming in vodka but he knows there's something alarming about that name—and then it clicks. *This is Mitzi.*

At that second, the front door swings open and Margaret bursts in wearing her cream-colored cashmere poncho over an ivory turtleneck dress and a very high pair of nude heels. Her red hair is windblown and her cheeks are bright pink. She is the most ravishing creature Drake has ever seen. He disentangles himself from Mitzi's arms and gets clumsily to his feet, knocking his shin against the coffee table.

He watches Margaret take in the scene: the leather sofa, the fire, Drake, Mitzi.

"Drake?" she says.

"Surprise," he says weakly. He hears footsteps on the stairs behind him, then he hears Kelley's voice.

"Margaret!" Kelley says. "Happy Stroll!" Then Kelley sees Mitzi and he does a double take. "Mitzi?"

In the two and a half years they've been seeing each other, Drake has never once witnessed Margaret Quinn lose her composure—but she comes close now. She shuts the front door with a little more force than is needed, and takes an extra moment turning around to face everyone. The source of her consternation seems to be Drake. Or Mitzi. Or what she perceives to have been happening between Drake and Mitzi.

"What exactly is going *on* here?" she asks.

Drake opens his mouth to explain, but no sound comes out. Mitzi starts to cry.

AVA

It starts out as just a ride home. Nathaniel takes his time driving up Main Street so they can both appreciate the lights on the trees and the shop windows—and then he heads to the right of Pacific National Bank onto Liberty Street. His radio plays classical Christmas music, "What Child Is This?" Ava nearly sings along, but she stops herself. Then she does sing, because singing is easier than talking. They'll be home in thirty seconds.

Nathaniel slows down as they approach Winter Street and says, "What if we drive to the end of Hinckley Lane and talk? It's still early. It's not even nine."

"Nathaniel," Ava says.

"What? I promise not to put the moves on you. I just want to talk to you, Ava."

She sighs. "Okay."

Nathaniel drives out Cliff Road, then takes a right onto Hinckley Lane—a dirt road that is very, very private, but at this time of year the police won't be out on the point checking for parkers. And even though it's Stroll weekend, most of the summer homes are dark and shuttered up.

Nathaniel pulls out to the edge of the bluff. Before them is Nantucket Sound, shining under a crescent moon. The crescent moon has always been Ava's favorite.

Nathaniel cuts the engine. It's quiet, and cold. "Do you want my jacket?" he asks.

"I'm fine," Ava says. "Jesus is keeping me warm."

"What?" Nathaniel says.

"My sweater," Ava says. She unzips her ski coat to reveal the Birthday Boy. Nathaniel throws his head back and laughs.

"That is classic!"

"I was wearing it at the bar," Ava says.

"I didn't notice what you were wearing at the bar," Nathaniel says. "I was blinded by your smile."

"Yeah, right," Ava says.

"I'm serious," Nathaniel says. He fiddles with the keys in the ignition for a second, then relaxes against his seat. "I miss you so much, Ava. I'm not going to lie—when I got to the Vineyard, I thought, Okay, new place, fresh start. I'll go out a couple of times, meet some women, start dating."

Ava feels a wave of unreasonable jealousy. "So," she asks, "did you date?"

"I did," he says. "Girl named Yvette, girl named Kendall."

"Yvette," Ava says. "Kendall."

"Nice girls, pretty girls, both unattached, both the right age. Yvette works as a bartender at Atria where I used to eat every night, and Kendall is the sales manager at Nell, this high-end women's clothing boutique in Edgartown. Kendall went to college with Kirsten Cabot, actually, so I knew of her before I got there..."

"Great," Ava says. She despises no one on the face of the planet more than Nathaniel's ex-girlfriend, Kirsten Cabot. Any friend of Kirsten's is an automatic enemy. "Why do I have to hear about this, Nathaniel?"

"Because they're great girls, not a thing wrong with them, and yet I only went out with them a couple times apiece before I lost interest. And as I told you earlier, I was working out in Chappy, which gave me more than enough time for self-reflection."

"And what did you conclude?" Ava asks.

"I concluded..." Here, Nathaniel swallows. He seems overcome. "I thought a lot about... *love* and what love is and what it would be like to be married, to spend a *lifetime* with someone. I mean, I know a lot of it is luck like my parents had, but some of it is also who you choose. My grandmother had this saying, 'Lust is great in the bedroom, but Like is better at breakfast, lunch, and dinner.'" His brow creases. "Or something like that."

"I get your point," Ava says.

"I *like* you, Ava. I enjoy being with you. And also you're pretty and you're sexy and I feel insane stupid mindless desire for you, but what I can't seem to find in anyone else is the friendship part, the breakfast, lunch, and dinner part. You're the coolest person I know. You're the person who gets me, you're the person who fits with me."

Ava is so taken aback by his words that she feels tears building. "We *were* great friends and we did get along and I do understand you. But I'm not sure *you* understand *me*. I'm not sure you know what I need. I need to feel like the only girl in the world. I need to feel like your sun and your moon. I need to be the woman who crowds your thoughts and makes you crazy. I am that person for Scott."

"Were you not *listening?*" he says. "You are that person for me, too. There's no way you can tell me all your feelings for me have died. There's no way Scott Skyler came in and replaced me in every way."

"Not in every way," Ava says. There are things she misses about Nathaniel—like the way he whistles Mozart when he sands wood, and his clear green eyes, and his irreverent sense of humor. Ava's relationship with Scott is solid and good and proper. They talk about school; they volunteer together; every day it feels like they're building something that's going to last. Ava feels safe with Scott. With Nathaniel, it always felt like she was dangling by her ankles outside a ten-story window. Did Nathaniel love her, did he not love her? The not-knowing, the never-being-sure was agony. It made Ava jealous and needy. It turned her into a person even *she* didn't like to hang out with.

"I want you to give me another chance," Nathaniel says. "I know you think people don't change..."

"People *don't* change," Ava says. "We are who we are, and then we keep becoming more and more ourselves."

"I know you think that," Nathaniel says. "I do listen when you talk. But I'm telling you, these last nine months on the Vineyard changed me. Or, okay, let's say they didn't *change* me—but I figured some shit out. And the number one thing I realized is that I want to be with you." He reached over and gently removed Ava's mitten until he was holding her small, cold hand. "I want to marry you, Ava."

Tears drop down her cheeks. She can't *believe* this is happening. And then, before she can figure out what to say, her phone starts to buzz. Scott: of course it's Scott, calling from the hospital. She should answer, but she absolutely cannot talk to Scott while she's sitting in Nathaniel's truck at the end of Hinckley Lane. She lets the call go.

She reclaims her hand and puts her mitten back on. These mittens were hand-knit for her by Mildred, one of the residents at Our Island Home. The best thing about the past year has been the joy she's found in playing for the elders, listening to them sing Bobby Darin and Cole Porter—and all the Rodgers and Hammerstein show tunes. Mildred's favorite is "Whatever Lola Wants," from *Damn Yankees;* she requests it every week. Ava loves that she and Scott volunteer together. Scott is vocal about his devotion. Ava never has to wonder.

She isn't going to trade that in. There *are* things about Nathaniel that she misses...okay, let's be painfully honest, there is some essential part of Nathaniel that she will always be hopelessly in love with.

"I'm confused," she admits. "I need you to take me home."

He nods, then turns the key and starts the engine. She's surprised that he's giving up so easily. She thought he might try to kiss her. She *wants* him to try to kiss her, she realizes—and how awful is *that?*

She wonders briefly if Roxanne is okay. She meant to listen for the sound of the Med Flight chopper, but being with Nathaniel distracted her. She doesn't think Scott left a message, which is unusual. She wonders if maybe he's angry with her. She worries that he somehow knows she's with Nathaniel right now. Is that possible? If he does know she's with Nathaniel, he will *not* be happy, but Ava will tell him Nathaniel needed some closure—and Scott will be understanding.

He is that good of a guy.

Nathaniel pulls up to the back of the Winter Street Inn and puts the truck in park. "I'd like to see you tomorrow night," he says.

"I'm busy tomorrow night," she says. "Black-tie thingy at the Whaling Museum."

"You're going with Scott?" he asks.

She nods.

He stares out the windshield at the lit window of Bart's bedroom. The door to Bart's bedroom is always kept open and the light always on—Kelley insists on this, as some kind of symbol—and there have been plenty of times when Ava has gone in and sat on Bart's bed and tried to feel from the energy in the room whether Bart is alive or dead. She always gets the sense that he is alive—but this might just be wishful thinking. She wants to share this with Nathaniel, except it would open a whole other can of worms.

He says, "I'd really like to kiss you good night. Can I kiss you good night?"

Every atom of her body is saying yes, and she even leans toward him a little, but then she thinks of Scott—who is, no doubt, still wearing the poufy tulle light-up Christmas tree sweater that he bought solely to please her.

"I have to go," she says, and she hops out of the truck, then hurries through the back door into the house.

She has never felt so torn in all her life. She needs to talk to her mother.

MARGARET

Many years earlier, at a CBS network retreat held at a farm in Millbrook, New York—back when Margaret had time for things like team-building and brainstorming—the facilitator asked everyone to pick two words to describe themselves.

Margaret chose *unflappable* and *busy*.

Busy certainly still applies.

Unflappable, not so much. And especially not tonight when she walks into the Winter Street Inn with one goal on her mind—to hold her precious granddaughter—and finds Drake and Mitzi together on the leather sofa.

Exactly *how* together, she can't quite tell.

She thinks: *Drake?* He told her he couldn't make it up this weekend. He had surgery scheduled and a mountain of paperwork. He was going to let paperwork trump the christening of Margaret's granddaughter. Drake has no children, essentially has no understanding of family, his father died in front of him at a Yankees game, heart attack. A man in the crowd, a doctor, performed CPR for half an hour trying to save him. Drake decided then and there he wanted to go into medicine. But he has no sense of family. How would Drake know how much it meant to Margaret to have him there? He's not in love with her. Love is too messy for Dr. Drake Carroll.

And yet—here he is. On the sofa with Mitzi. Margaret realizes that Mitzi must be on Nantucket for the baptism. Did Kelley *invite* her? No, he looks almost as surprised as Margaret to find Drake and Mitzi sitting together on the sofa in front of the fire.

Margaret shuts the front door, trying to summon the consummate professional who has broadcast the results of six presidential elections. If she can handle announcing the name of the future leader of the free world, then she can handle this.

"What exactly is going *on* here?" she asks. She sounds like a schoolmarm.

Drake is at a loss for words and Mitzi starts bawling.

Kelley says, "Mitzi, what are you doing here? I thought we agreed..."

"I know!" she says. "I couldn't help myself. I just miss him so much."

Margaret softens. Poor Mitzi. If Patrick or Kevin had been taken prisoner in Afghanistan, how would Margaret function? Would she be able to face the nation every night and deliver the news? Certainly not. She'd take a leave of absence. She would, like Mitzi, be a basket case.

Drake holds his perfect surgeon's hands in the air in a gesture of innocence. He looks at Margaret beseechingly. *Drake is here. He put whatever was on his plate aside to show up to surprise me.* She softens further.

Kelley says, "Mitzi, can I see you in the dining room, please?"

Mitzi stands. "Thank you again," she says to Drake.

"My pleasure," Drake says.

Mitzi follows Kelley into the dining room—where, apparently, the lashings are to be administered.

Drake collects Margaret in his arms. He whispers in her ear, "I didn't know who that was. I was working, and she walked right in, plopped down next to me on the sofa, and started crying."

"It's okay," Margaret says. "I understand. She's like that."

Drake then lays a kiss on Margaret that makes her wobble in her heels. Wow, the man can kiss! He slices through to the center of her with . . . well, with surgical precision.

She's in the middle of some kind of ecstasy when she hears Kevin's voice. "Hey, Mom!"

She and Drake separate—reluctantly.

"Darling," she says. She kisses her son on the cheek; it's been a few days since he's shaved. "How is everything going?" Isabelle appears behind him. She looks exhausted.

"Margaret," she says, and they kiss on both cheeks. "Can I bring you some *gougères?*"

Drake says, "I'm taking Margaret to dinner at 56 Union."

Yes, Margaret thinks. She'll ask Wendy to stick them in a dark corner where no one will recognize her, and she'll devour a big bowl of the curried mussels and a big glass of chardonnay. She's starving.

The front door opens and Jennifer strolls in, holding a paper bag. She looks dazed.

"Jennifer!" Margaret says. "My lovely girl." Margaret and Jennifer have always had a good relationship, and Margaret has been extra solicitous since Patrick has gone to jail. Margaret sends Jennifer flowers every month, she arranged for the boys to attend a Red Sox game and sit in the owner's box, and for Christmas, Margaret is flying Jennifer to Canyon Ranch in Arizona for three days while Jennifer's mother keeps the boys in San Francisco.

Jennifer gives Margaret a squeeze. She says, "I have wine. Would you like a glass?"

"Sure," Margaret says.

Drake says, "I'm taking Margaret out to dinner."

"That's right," Margaret says. She checks her Cartier tank watch. This is the very same watch that sent Mitzi into an apoplectic fit the Christmas before—because it was a gift to Margaret from Kelley when Ava was born, and Margaret still chooses to wear it on the air. "We should go."

"Don't you want to see the baby first, Mom?" Kevin asks.

"Is she awake?" Margaret asks.

"She's in her crib, kicking around," Kevin says.

Well, Margaret isn't going to miss an opportunity to hold her granddaughter. She turns to Jennifer, "Are the boys here?"

"Upstairs, playing PS4 with Grandpa, I'm pretty sure," Jennifer says. "You can see them in the morning."

"Grandpa is in the dining room with Mitzi," Margaret says.

"Mitzi?" Isabelle says.

Margaret smiles diplomatically. "I'm going to give Genevieve one kiss," she says. "And then we'll go."

"I'll come with you," Drake says. "I'd like to see Genevieve."

"Really?" Margaret says. Drake has never shown anything beyond polite interest in Genevieve before. But he dutifully follows Margaret into the back of the inn toward the baby's nursery.

The nursery is lit by only one scallop shell night-light, which casts a buttery glow over the giraffe-and-umbrella-themed nursery. Isabelle grew up with a special fondness for *les girafes et les parapluies*. Although Margaret initially found the combination a little random, the nursery has turned out to be quite charming.

She can hear Genevieve cooing, and when Margaret peers into the crib, the baby is smiling up at her.

"Hello, beautiful doll," Margaret whispers. She reaches in and scoops her up.

Baby baby baby. There is nothing Margaret has experienced in this life that compares to holding her grandchildren, and especially this little girl, who is just a little lighter and a little sweeter than the boys were. She smells like lavender, and as Margaret nuzzles her cheek and her tiny perfect ear, she marvels at how soft her skin is. She kisses and kisses her. She can't ever remember feeling this enamored with her own kids. With Patrick, she was overwhelmed, the twenty-four-hour-a-day nursing sucked away all her energy, and then she got mastitis in her left breast. Kelley's mother, Frances, had still been alive and she had come to stay with Kelley and Margaret in their railroad apartment on 121st Street, and offered unsolicited advice on the hour.

Suffice it to say, Margaret's memories of Patrick were not as delicious as this.

Kevin had been easier because at least with him, Margaret had known what she was doing. But Kevin had suffered from reflux—everything she fed him came back up and the whole apartment smelled like sour milk—plus, she'd had a two-year-old to take care of.

And when Ava was born, Margaret had been working full-time at WCBS in New York and every day at home with Ava was a day that Margaret feared she was going to be replaced.

It is *so much better* to be a grandparent. Margaret can't believe how much better it is.

"I want to eat her," Margaret says to Drake. "I want to gobble her up."

"May I?" Drake says, and he holds his hands out.

Margaret is surprised; he's never asked to hold the baby before. But of course he operates on babies this age and younger all the time. He takes the baby and cradles her expertly in his arms, just like he does it every day of his life.

"Does it feel different?" she asks. "Holding a healthy baby?"

Drake smiles down at Genevieve. "No," he says. "All babies are equally miraculous."

Margaret loves this answer so much she feels tears prick her eyes. So much for unflappable.

She says, "Let's give her back to her parents so we can go to dinner." The most miraculous thing of all about grandchildren: They can be handed back to their parents at any time!

"Okay," Drake says. Margaret follows him, as he gently bounces Genevieve in his arms, out into the hallway.

"Mommy?"

Margaret turns around. She may be a grandmother, but the sound of her children's voices calling her *Mommy* is indelibly printed in her mind. Ava is waiting at the back door. She, too, looks dazed.

"Darling," Margaret says, and she goes to give her daughter a hug. "How are you?"

Ava looks at Margaret with big eyes—then she notices Drake, and she regains some composure. "Hey, Drake."

"Hey there, Ava," Drake says. "Happy holidays."

"Is everything okay, darling?" Margaret asks. "How was the caroling party?"

"Oh," Ava says, "long story. Do you have time to talk right now? Or… would you rather wait until morning?"

"Let's wait until morning," Margaret says, though she can tell Ava is carrying something she'd like to unload right now. But Margaret is starving and Drake has been patient enough. "Tomorrow morning will be perfect."

KELLEY

Peace on earth, good will toward men. He has repeated the words so often, he's starting to feel like Linus van Pelt.

This was an easier tenet to live by before Mitzi showed up unannounced and, in typical Mitzi fashion, tried to throw herself at Dr. Drake Carroll!

When Kelley gets Mitzi into the dining room alone, he says, "What is *wrong* with you?"

She says, "I had to come. I had to be back in the house where we raised him."

Kelley wants to yell; he wants to fight. Only now, a year later, can Kelley fully acknowledge how Mitzi broke his heart, how she blindsided him. He had been incredulous at first: An affair with George the Santa Claus *for twelve years?* It was so absurd that Kelley had a hard time comprehending it; plus, there had been the immediate distraction of Margaret. For a few days, Kelley had thought the world had resynchronized so that he and Margaret could get back together.

But that idea evaporated with the new year. Margaret Quinn was Margaret Quinn—too important, too busy, too citified. She had grown beyond Kelley; she had no interest in running an inn on Nantucket. She had been incredibly kind to float him a seven-figure "loan" he would never have to repay, and to come to the inn so often, bringing sixteen rooms of guests in her wake. Drake is a much better match for Margaret, even if she refuses to acknowledge it.

Most of the reason Kelley is so upset Mitzi is here is because it hurts to see her.

It hurts.

At least she didn't bring George.

"You can't just show up here unannounced," Kelley says.

"I want to see his room," she says. "I want to look at his things."

Kelley sighs. "Okay," he says. "Five minutes, then you have to go."

Mitzi follows Kelley into the back of the inn—ahead of them, Margaret and Drake are headed to the nursery—but Kelley takes a left down the short hallway that leads to Bart's room.

Kelley says, "I keep the door open and the light on day and night so it's ready for him when he gets back."

"You do?" Mitzi says. She seems touched by this. Her eyes fill with tears. "Because he *is* coming back, right?"

"Yes, Mitzi," Kelley says, "he's coming back." He gently touches Mitzi's back, ushering her into the room.

She sits on Bart's bed. She stops crying; something about the room calms her. Mitzi's lips are moving. It takes Kelley a second, but then he realizes she's saying their son's name, over and over.

Bart Bart Bart Bart Bart.

He sits down on the bed next to her and takes her hand.

AVA

Scott didn't leave a voicemail, and when Ava calls him back—once she's safely ensconced in her bedroom—he doesn't answer.

It's nearly midnight before he sends her a text: *Still at hospital.*

She thinks, *Still at hospital?*

She should go be with him. He's been there nearly three hours. What could be taking so long?

Hmmmmm, Roxanne, she thinks. Then she falls asleep.

SATURDAY,
DECEMBER 5

JENNIFER

She wakes up hungover, the result of drinking an entire bottle of chardonnay by herself, and then chasing that with not one, not two, but *three* Ativan.

She feels so rotten that she has no choice but to take an oxy. Six left. She heads down to the kitchen.

"Coffee?" she says to Kelley. She ekes out half a smile. The oxy takes exactly twelve minutes to kick in, and she will hit her absolute high in an hour.

Kelley pours her a cup and reaches for the bottle of Bailey's, looking first to her for approval. She says, "Why not?"

Kelley winks and hands her the magic elixir. He's making the guests of the inn blueberry cornmeal pancakes and applewood smoked bacon while Isabelle whips up made-to-order omelettes. Jennifer loads three plates with pancakes for the boys and then lures them away from the PS4 long enough to eat them at the kitchen counter.

She says, "We're going into town in fifteen minutes."

"Not me," Barrett says.

"Me either," Pierce says, syrup dripping down his chin.

Jennifer takes a sustaining sip of her coffee, and regards her sons. The one who is taking Patrick's absence the hardest is Barrett, the oldest. His strategy for coping is to vent on the only parent left...Jennifer. Barrett has told Jennifer that he hates her; he has said, "I wish you were the one who had gone to prison." It's awful, soul-crushing stuff, and Jennifer steels herself every time she's in the same room with him. He's angry, and humiliated, and he misses his dad. When Jennifer says, "Listen, I know you're angry and humiliated, and that you miss your dad," Barrett says, "I don't care about Dad. It's you. I hate *you*."

Pierce is wrapped in a bubble of narcissism. He only cares about how Patrick's absence affects *him*. For example, he's pissed that Patrick missed a season of coaching lacrosse, and blames Patrick for his team not making the playoffs, when in past years, with Patrick at the helm, they won three championships in a row. Jaime, the youngest, is the only one, other than Jennifer, who acknowledges a sad, gaping hole. Jennifer wakes up three nights out of four with him clinging to her, like a barnacle on her boat.

"I'll go into town with you, Mom," Jaime says.

"I'll get you cocoa at the pharmacy," she says. "And Santa is coming in on the noon boat."

"There is no Santa," Barrett says.

"Hey," Jennifer says with a warning look. "Those who don't believe, don't receive. No Santa means no Madden 16 and no surfboard."

"Yeah," Jaime says.

The oxy tends to make Jennifer combative and impatient, but even so, she doesn't feel like forcing the older two boys to come to town. The last thing she wants is two truculent kids to drag through the crowds. For Stroll, Main Street is closed to traffic and it becomes one giant party. Ostensibly, shopping is the main activity, although there are carolers singing and a buzzing anticipation of Santa's arrival by Coast Guard boat. All of the restaurants serve holiday cocktails. One year, Jennifer and Patrick secured window seats at Arno's and they proceeded to get quite cheerful drinking Christmas martinis.

Jennifer decides she would like some adult company, someone to keep an eye on Jaime while she shops. She needs a new dress for the black-tie event that evening. She's lost fourteen pounds since Patrick went to jail; she is now a size 00, and all of her clothes hang on her. She hasn't been out anywhere in almost a year. Tonight, therefore, is kind of a big deal, and she would like something new. But there is no sign of Margaret or Drake, and Ava's door is shut tight. Kevin is... on baby duty. Jennifer finds him in the nursery, giving Genevieve a bottle.

"Hey, I'm taking Jaime into town," she says. "Would you and Genevieve like to join us?"

He blinks at her. He looks exhausted, or maybe he's just feeling the effects of the Jameson. "Sure," he says. "That's a great idea. I'll take Genevieve on an outing, give Isabelle time to finish up with breakfast and start on the rooms. Then when I get back, I'll take over the rooms and she and Genevieve can nap."

It's a full hour before Kevin and Genevieve are ready to go, by which time Jennifer is panting like a rabid dog. She takes another oxy. Five left. Certainly that will be enough to get through the rest of the weekend. She'll have to call Megan on Monday for more. Either that or be done.

Be done, she decides. She will be done with the oxy on Monday.

She doesn't like to consider how many times she has decided to be done.

What had taken Kevin so long? Well, Isabelle declared that she wanted Genevieve to have a bath before she went into town, and giving a bath to a squirming three-month-old is a process, as Jennifer well recalls. She actually volunteered to help Kevin, but Kevin is one of those parents who prefer to do everything himself, including clean between each toe and the outer rims of Genevieve's delicate ears, and once Genevieve is dry, naked on the towel, he digs at her navel with a Q-tip, which actually makes Jennifer release a sigh of impatience.

"You can go, Jen," Kevin said. "We'll meet up with you."

"No, no," Jennifer said. "I'd like to go together."

After the baby was dried and lotioned and powdered, there was the bundling of layers. And *then,* when Genevieve was completely swaddled, she made a scrunched-up, determined-looking face and Kevin said, "Uh-oh, oh *no!*" And Genevieve pooped loudly, necessitating the removal of all the layers, a serious diaper change, and then relayering. Jennifer forgot how long it takes to get anything done with an infant—and how much paraphernalia one needs. When Kevin is finally ready, his shoulder bag is packed up with diapers, wipes, an extra outfit, pacifiers, two bottles of expressed milk, a rattle, a plush toy, and a blanket.

The second oxy has given the whole world a surreal shimmer. It's terrible how much Jennifer enjoys not being in her right mind. She can tell, however, that Jaime is antsy and that staying behind to play video games with his brothers is probably looking pretty enticing, but he hangs tight with Mom, exerting only the subtlest arm tugs and exhalations of exasperation.

Finally, Kevin has the baby secured in the Björn and the bag ready to go.

"Christmas Stroll, here we come," he says.

Town is packed. Jennifer can't believe how packed it is. There are *thousands* of people milling about. The weather is overcast with very light snow flurries. It's perfect Stroll weather. All of the lights on the trees are lit and the shop windows glow. There is a group of Victorian carolers singing "God Rest Ye Merry, Gentlemen" on the street in front of Murray's Toggery. Jennifer stops to listen. She yearns for Patrick. It's eleven o'clock in the morning, which means he's finishing up at the gym, and it's Saturday, which means he works lunch shift in the cafeteria, a job that pays three dollars an hour. (As Patrick says, at his other job, he made three dollars in the time it took him to blow his nose.)

Genevieve starts to cry. Kevin says, "Let's walk."

Jennifer says, "I promised Jaime a cocoa from the pharmacy."

"By all means," Kevin says.

The Nantucket Pharmacy has an old-fashioned lunch counter and the best cocoa on the island. It's served in a thick ceramic mug with a mountain of whipped cream and a candy cane garnish. Jaime perches on a stool and Jennifer snaps a photo of him before he demolishes his drink. The only thing she has excelled at since Patrick has gone to prison is documenting every little moment. Kevin wanders the aisles, gently bouncing Genevieve until she falls asleep against his chest.

"Success," he whispers.

The door to the pharmacy jingles and suddenly Jennifer feels a hand on her shoulder. In addition to everything else, the oxy makes her paranoid; she whips around.

It's George.

"George!" Jennifer says. "Hi!" She gives him a hug, then looks behind him for Mitzi, but he appears to be alone.

"She's back at the hotel," George says. "Sleeping it off."

Jennifer composes what she hopes is a sympathetic expression. "I'm a bit hungover myself," she admits. But she knows that she was nowhere close to as drunk as Mitzi last night. Mitzi was a train wreck. Jennifer wonders briefly if she also takes pills.

George turns to Kevin. "Kevin, how are you?"

Kevin nods. Jennifer isn't sure what kind of relationship Kevin has with George, if any. Mitzi reached out to Jennifer right after Patrick was sentenced, and Jennifer wasn't in a position to rebuff her. However, somehow, over the course of the past year, Jennifer has found herself becoming the conduit between Mitzi and the rest of the Quinns. Mitzi asks for updates on how the family is faring and Jennifer, unwilling and really unable to lie, provides them.

Kevin says, "Oh, can't complain."

George takes a peek inside the Björn. "Here's the angel, then? What a beauty."

Kevin grins. "That she is."

The door to the pharmacy jingles again and a redheaded woman wanders in. "Hey, George!" she calls out.

George checks his watch. "Right on time, Mary Rose," he says. He winks at Jennifer and Kevin. "I agreed to buy this young lady some lunch. I'll see you kids tomorrow morning at the church."

"See you then," Kevin says.

George steers the redhead, Mary Rose, to a stool at the end of the counter.

Jaime slurps the last of his cocoa. Jennifer urges him up—and out.

When they're on the street, she turns to Kevin. "I have to apologize. It's my fault Mitzi and George showed up here this weekend. Mitzi asked a month or so ago when you were baptizing the baby, and I told her."

"Jen, it's okay," Kevin says. "I mean, Mitzi was my step-mother for more than twenty years. I would have invited her myself, but Dad . . ."

"Yeah," Jennifer says.

"I didn't feel like I could invite Mitzi back into his sphere," Kevin says. "But I'm glad she's coming. Especially with Bart missing...it feels like we should all be together."

"Okay, good," Jennifer says. She knows that Kevin and Ava and Bart all think of her like a sister, but she's aware that she wasn't born a Quinn. She would never want to overstep her bounds as an in-law.

They proceed down the street, dodging and weaving among the fur coats. Jennifer wonders briefly about the redhead George is taking to lunch while Mitzi is "sleeping it off," when suddenly she sees the sign for Murray's Liquors, and she gasps.

"Oh my gosh, Kevin!" she says.

"Oh my gosh, what?" Kevin says.

Jennifer stops dead in her tracks, nearly causing a ten-person pileup behind her. Kevin moves her a few steps out of the way. "What's wrong?" he says.

She can't decide what to tell him. The fact is, Jennifer forgot about seeing Norah Vale. Or didn't forget so much as *lost* the fact; that often happened when she took Ativan. She had thought of it briefly that morning as Kelley was making breakfast, although obviously it wasn't anything Jennifer would ever mention in front of Isabelle. She wonders now if it was even real, or if she'd imagined it. She wonders if the woman she saw was Norah Vale, or only a woman who greatly resembled Norah. After all, the woman hadn't acknowledged Jennifer or shown any flicker of recognition. She had sniffed at Jennifer—maybe in disgust at being mistakenly called Norah. Jennifer can't bring herself to alarm Kevin for no reason. Their family has too much going on as it is.

"Oh, nothing," she says.

"What?" Kevin says. "Tell me."

"It's nothing," Jennifer says. "I just remembered that I need to shop for a dress."

AVA

Ava sleeps late, a bad habit she only indulges in when it's a weekend and she's not staying over at Scott's; he insists on rising with the dawn and running six miles, regardless of the weather.

She rolls over to check the clock. It's five of eleven. That's pretty pathetic, even for her. She needs to get her butt out of bed, find coffee, eat whatever her father has left over, and then start helping Kevin and Isabelle with the rooms.

But first, she looks at her phone. Against her will, she finds herself hoping for a text from Nathaniel. But instead, there's another missed call—no message—and a text from Scott that says: *I'm headed to MGH with Roxanne.*

Ava sits bolt upright in bed. "What?" she shouts.

She calls Scott immediately. He answers on the sixth ring. "Hello?" He sounds exhausted, but Ava doesn't care.

"You're in *Boston?*" she says. "With *Roxanne?* What *for,* Scott? I'm...flummoxed here! Why did you go to Boston with Roxanne?"

"She got Med-Flighted early this morning, and I took the first ferry, then rented a car," he says. "The ankle is badly broken, she needs surgery. She's scared, Ava, like crying-scared, little-girl-scared, and she doesn't have anyone else. Her mother is in California, her brother's in Denver, and she says she doesn't have any close girlfriends to ask for help."

Ava bites her tongue. Roxanne doesn't have any close girlfriends because she isn't the type of woman another woman trusts. *Crying-scared, little-girl-scared?* This is, possibly, the most absurd phrase Ava has ever heard come out of Scott's mouth, but she can picture exactly the way Roxanne tugged on Scott's heartstrings. She acted like a fourth grader with a skinned knee and Scott was unable to resist. Of *course* he took the first ferry, of *course* he rented a car! Ava has to take a moment to center herself. Roxanne broke her ankle; she can't walk. She has no family on Nantucket, no close friends. If Ava had broken her ankle, her father and brother would have been there; Shelby would have been there. Scott would have been there.

"When are you coming home?" Ava asks. "You'll be home by six, right?" At six o'clock, the entire Quinn family is going to the Festival of Trees party, thrown by the Nantucket Historical Association at the Whaling Museum. It is the premier event of Christmas Stroll weekend.

"Ava…" Scott says.

"Don't tell me," Ava says. "Do not."

"She's scheduled to go into surgery between three and four this afternoon," Scott says. "They don't know how long that will take, but I need to be here when she wakes up. That's Roxanne's main concern. She doesn't want to come out of the anesthesia and be alone."

Ava's main concern is losing her date to the Festival of Trees—which isn't quite in the same category. And yet, her overriding feeling is that Scott is *her* boyfriend, *not* Roxanne's, and hence Scott's rightful place tonight is by Ava's side.

"So what you're telling me is that you're not getting back tonight," Ava says.

"Probably not," Scott says.

"What about tomorrow?" Ava asks. "You'll be back in time for the *baptism,* right?" Her voice can now carry as much indignation as she wants. Scott may feel okay canceling on her, but he can't ditch on baby Genevieve.

"I should be," he says. "I think I should wait and see how it goes."

Ava is silent.

"I'm so sorry, Ava. I don't know how I got myself into this position."

Ava knows—and it's why she loves him. He's a good person. He would never leave Roxanne, or anyone else, to face surgery scared and alone.

"It's okay," Ava says.

"It's *not* okay," Scott says. "I *hate* to let you down. I can assure you I do *not* want to be sitting here at Mass General when I could be lying in bed with you. And I'm even more upset about missing tonight. When I close my eyes, I can picture how gorgeous you're going to look in that green dress."

The green velvet with the slit up one leg, purchased on a weekend that Ava and Scott went to visit Margaret in Manhattan. It is a spectacular dress that she will wear with the diamond circle necklace Margaret bought her last Christmas, and a pair of black silk Louboutin heels, also a gift from Margaret.

Scott is going to miss it!

Briefly, Ava thinks of calling Nathaniel and asking him to go. Then that thought evaporates and is replaced by Ava wondering how she could ever be so wicked.

"It's okay about tonight," she says. "I understand."

"Do you?" he says.

"Just try to get home first thing tomorrow," she says. "The baptism is important."

"I'll do everything in my power, Ava, I promise," Scott says. "I love you so much."

"And I love you," she says.

MARGARET

Drake is different. He is playful and relaxed and wholly focused on her. He hasn't checked his email once that she's noticed—but is this possible? Drake prides himself on being available any instant that he's not actually in the operating room.

She says, "Have you checked in at the hospital?"

He kisses her under the ear and a delicious shiver runs through her. "Nope. Jim Hahn is covering for me."

"You got Jim to cover for you on a *weekend?*" Margaret asks. Jim Hahn, the only surgical colleague Drake completely trusts to cover his patients, also happens to be the father of five, and his weekends are sacred.

"I called in a favor," Drake says. "I wanted to be here."

"I just…" Margaret doesn't quite know how to express her feelings. She had thought, when Drake so brusquely turned down her invitation, saying he had *too much paperwork* of all things, that he simply didn't want to come. And as disappointed as Margaret was, she understood. Drake led a regimented life: the hospital, his patients, his colleagues. Margaret didn't blame him for not wanting to dive into the Quinn family stew.

And yet here he is, telling her he wants to be here.

He kisses the tip of her nose. "I love you, Margaret."

Her eyes widen and she again wishes for *unflappable*. Dr.

Drake Carroll has just said the three words she was certain she would never hear come out of his mouth. She had been so certain that she had stopped hoping.

"You love me?" she says, making sure.

"I love you."

"You just said it again."

"Because it's true. I love you. I got Jim to cover and I came here to surprise you because I love you, Margaret Quinn."

She rolls onto her back and stares at the ceiling. The last first time a man told her he loved her she was twenty-three years old and it was Kelley Quinn.

Drake clears his throat. "Do you... love *me?*"

"You know what?" Margaret says. "I believe I do."

Now, not only is Drake different, Margaret is different. They are different together. They are in love, they've said it out loud, acknowledged it, owned it. And Margaret can't believe it but it feels just as wonderful as it did the first time, with Kelley. Or maybe it feels better because this second time, at age sixty, it's a gift. When Margaret was twenty-three living in a studio in the East Village and going to grad school at NYU, she had fully expected that love would come to her. She would get married and have children. But now, nearly forty years later, to get a second chance seems miraculous.

Love changes everything. Margaret and Drake lie in bed until almost noon, then Margaret takes a long, hot shower (during which time, she's sure, Drake checks his email). They get dressed, Margaret puts on a hat and her Tom Ford sunglasses, and they head into town, hand in hand.

"Wow," Drake says when they reach the top of Main Street. "Mob scene. Are you sure you're ready for this?"

"I'll keep my sunglasses on," she says. "No one will recognize me unless I want them to."

"Spoken with confidence," Drake says.

They pop into a number of shops, all of them crowded—Stephanie's gift shop, Mitchell's Book Corner, Erica Wilson. All of the shops offer hot cider or cocoa, and some have hors d'oeuvres. At the Dane Gallery, there is a full-blown charcuterie platter laid out, and Drake digs in while Margaret ogles the handblown glass ornaments. She loves one that is a clear globe with a detailed toy soldier suspended inside. She says, "I love these ornaments, but I can never manage to put up a tree."

"They make wonderful gifts," the saleslady says.

Margaret turns to Drake. "Do you put up a tree?"

"What do you think?" he asks, popping a piece of prosciutto into his mouth.

"I think you're lucky if you find time to open the three cards you receive," she says.

"I get more than three," Drake says. "Some years."

"I could buy one for Darcy, but she's too young to appreciate it. I could get one for Lee Kramer, but he's Jewish. My kids have too much Christmas paraphernalia in their house as it is...except for Jennifer. And Jennifer has exquisite taste. Yes, I'll get it for Jennifer."

"Good idea," Drake says. He smears a cracker with an obscene amount of pâté, and Margaret worries he's going to ruin his lunch.

"Although, I've gotten a lot of gifts for Jennifer this year," Margaret says. "I don't want the other kids to resent her..."

A woman standing just behind Margaret says, "Excuse me, aren't you Margaret Quinn, from the *Today* show?"

Margaret hangs the ornament back up where she found it. She has been recognized—sort of. "I'm afraid I'm not familiar with the *Today* show," she says with a wink.

The woman, who is tall with a rather long nose, doesn't get the joke. "It's on every morning," she says.

"Wonderful!" Margaret says. She pulls Drake away from the duck-and-apple sausage and leads him toward the door.

Margaret suggests stopping at Murray's Liquors to get a bottle of champagne to chill and drink before they go out that night.

She says, "I'll be in full Margaret-Quinn-of-the-*Today*-show mode this evening, so it'll be nice to have a little quiet time first."

Drake picks a couple of cigars out of the store's humidor. "I'm going to see if Kelley wants to smoke one of these beauties with me later. Engage in some male bonding, celebrate the baptism of his granddaughter, that kind of thing."

Margaret is starving, but the food tent in the parking lot of the Stop & Shop seems like too much chaos, and so Margaret leads Drake down a narrow cobblestone alley toward the Starlight Theatre & Cafe.

"Is this where we saw that Nantucket slideshow?" Drake asks.

"Good memory," Margaret says. This past summer, Margaret dragged Drake to a slideshow featuring the photographs of Cary Hazlegrove, in hopes that it would make Drake fall in love with Nantucket. He seems pretty smitten with the island right now. "The café has great chowder and they serve a BLT with too much bacon, which is exactly how I like it," Margaret says.

They step in and Margaret makes her way past the movie line toward the bar. There are two empty seats on the end— perfect perfection!

But then Margaret stops. Also sitting at the bar is Mitzi, by herself, with a glass of wine in front of her.

Margaret does an about-face.

"Your special friend is here," Margaret says, poking

Drake in the ribs. Margaret understands why Mitzi came to Nantucket this weekend, but she draws the line at including Mitzi in her romantic lunch.

"Come on," she says to Drake. "Let's go to the Club Car."

MITZI

When she wakes up in their room at the Castle, George is gone. Mitzi's head feels like it's been bashed in with a brick, and the inside of her mouth is so dry it feels like it's coated with sand. She reaches for the bottle of water next to the bed, but it's empty. She will have to stand up.

Then, she remembers the fight.

It was her first full-blown screaming, yelling, and crying fight with George, a fight loud enough to bring the hotel's night manager to their door to see if everything was okay.

It started when Mitzi stumbled home from the inn, dropped off out front by Kelley, and found George having a Scotch in the bar with the redhead from the Holiday House Tour. Mitzi had gone into the bar to get herself a nightcap that she didn't need, but she had *not* expected to find her partner chatting up another woman. Rosemary, or whatever her name was. Mary Rose.

Mitzi managed to hold it together—sort of—in the public space of the bar. George looked *extremely flustered* when she tapped him on the shoulder, and he was quick to explain the *enormous coincidence:* Mary Rose was also staying at the hotel, and the two of them had ended up there for dinner.

"Since I didn't hear from you," George said.

Mitzi had skipped dinner—but for the past year, this was often how it went.

"How did you get home from the inn?" George asked. "Did you walk?"

"Kelley dropped me," Mitzi admitted.

George nodded curtly, then called for his check. He made their excuses to Mary Rose and they marched down the hall to their room in silence. Once they were inside, Mitzi lost her temper.

She said, "Sorry to interrupt your little date."

"It wasn't a date," George said. "I told you, we both happened to be having dinner at the bar. It was a coincidence."

"You have now used the word 'coincidence' twice," Mitzi said. "Which tells me it wasn't a coincidence. I think a more honest way to describe what happened is that you and Mary Rose had so much fun chatting on the house tour that you decided to go to dinner together afterward." Mitzi didn't like how thick her voice sounded; she was slurring her words, which undermined the validity of the point she was trying to make.

"You were at the inn a long time," George said. "And I didn't hear from you."

"Did you *call* me?" Mitzi asked. "Did you *text* me?"

"No," George said. "No, I did not. Because I was trying to give you the time and space to do whatever it was you wanted to do at the inn."

It was then that Mitzi had spun out of control. She screamed and cried and called George a fat, insensitive bastard. She told him he couldn't understand her pain because he had never had children; she accused him of going out and seeking a fun time with a stranger because Mitzi wasn't fun anymore and George was tired of living with someone so miserable.

George had said, "I love you, Mitzi. But it was enjoyable, I admit, to have a regular conversation. Mary Rose was *nice* to me. Do you know how long it's been since you were *nice* to me?"

George might as well have poured lighter fluid on the hot coals of her anger. She *screamed*—with words, then unintelligible words, then she just made noise for the sake of making noise. Then…well, the truth is, she doesn't remember anything else except for the knock on the door. The night manager.

George said to the man, "My lovely Mrs. Claus here has a son who is serving our country in Afghanistan, and we've had some bad news."

The night manager said he of course understood and he asked if there was anything he could do. George assured him there was nothing *anyone* could do, but that they would quiet down. "Please accept our apologies," George said. "I'm sure we're disturbing the other guests. They probably think someone is being murdered in here."

The night manager laughed uncertainly and George closed the door.

He then turned to Mitzi with that look on his face, the same look Kelley sometimes gave her which said: *Well, I hope you're happy. Now the whole world knows you're crazy.*

He'd said, in a voice she found patronizing, "Would you like me to draw you a bath, darling?"

"No," she'd said tersely. She lay down on the bed. She was tired, too tired to even take off her shoes. "No, I don't think so."

Now, Mitzi is undressed—or, at least, stripped to her underwear and T-shirt—and George is gone. Mitzi swings her legs to the floor and hoists herself up. She staggers to the bathroom for water, and then she digs her phone out of her coat pocket. There is nothing from George.

She texts: *Where are you?*

As she waits for a response, she checks the room for a note. She finds nothing.

Bart Bart Bart Bart Bart.

Her phone dings. The text from George says: *I'm at lunch on Main Street with Mary Rose.*

Mitzi blinks. Does the text *really* say that? She can't be sure; her headache is so bad she might have brain damage. She reads it again. George is at lunch with Mary Rose.

She texts back: *Seriously?*

He texts back: *Yes, seriously. Finishing up. Should be back to room in 20 minutes.*

Mitzi is filled with confused emotion. What she needs more than anything right now is a friend to either confirm that her anger is justified or talk her off the ledge. But Mitzi no longer has any friends. Those she had a year ago, she left behind here on Nantucket. She hasn't made a single woman friend in Lenox. The girls who work at the millinery shop for George don't speak English and all of the other women George knows in town are friends of his ex-wife, Patti.

Mitzi sits on her bed and brings up her email on her phone. Should she write to Gayle, she wonders, or Yasmin? She has never broached any topic with her pen pals other than their missing sons. But her issues with George are not unrelated. After some contemplation, she chooses Yasmin. Gayle has been happily married for thirty years and she's a fundamentalist Christian; Mitzi isn't sure if Gayle would understand that Mitzi left her husband after a twelve-year affair with their Santa Claus. Whereas Yasmin, living in Brooklyn, would have seen everything.

To: mamayasmin@yahoo.com
From: queenie229@gmail.com
Subject: Man trouble

Yasmin, hi—

I know I've shared with you that my partner's name is
George and that George is not Bart's father. The truth is
that I was married to Kelley Quinn, Bart's father, for
twenty-one years but for twelve of those years I was con-
ducting a one-weekend-a-year affair at Christmastime
with the man who served as our Santa Claus. That man is
George. Last year, shortly before Bart deployed, I decided
to leave Kelley for George, and I moved with George
across the Commonwealth to Lenox, Massachusetts.

I'm beginning to think that I've made a monumen-
tal mistake. Possibly, the stress of Bart going to war
clouded my judgment. I should have forsaken George
and clung to Kelley; instead, I did the opposite.

It has been a miserable year for me, not only
because of Bart, but because I have been living with a
man I do not love.

I do not love George.

Mitzi stares at the screen of her phone. She can't believe
she has just written those words.

The words are true: She doesn't love George. She doesn't
care that George is having lunch with Mary Rose. She's
relieved that he's found a friend because this means there is
no pressure for Mitzi to be cheerful or play along at enjoying
the activities of Stroll weekend.

Yasmin, I am writing to ask for your advice. What
should I do? The man I really love is Bart's father,

Kelley—but I have done so much damage to the relationship that I fear it can't be repaired. Please let me know your thoughts. I know we have never met in person, but right now you are the woman I feel closest to because of our shared sorrow.

God Bless Our Troops,

Mitzi

Mitzi presses Send, then she pulls on her jeans and goes to the bathroom to brush her teeth. Her hair is beyond help; she will have to wear a hat. She applies moisturizer, but no makeup. She hasn't bothered with makeup in months and months; it's pointless.

George will be back in the room in twenty minutes but Mitzi won't be here. She is going out to get a drink.

KELLEY

Saturday is *very busy,* which is a good thing because it keeps Kelley from thinking too much about Mitzi.

Kelley wakes up at six o'clock and heads to the kitchen to brew coffee and get started on breakfast. He cooks three pounds of bacon on the griddle, some soft, some crispy, and mixes the batter for his famous tri-berry cornmeal pancakes. Mr. Blount, room 7, comes down for coffee at six thirty and a few seconds later, Isabelle appears to do the mise-en-place for her omelette service.

Kelley says, "How did the baby sleep?"

Isabelle waggles her hand. "*Comme ci, comme ça.* She wakes up twice."

"You should go back to bed and make Kevin come out here to cook breakfast," Kelley says.

Isabelle laughs. "Eggshell omelettes."

Busy, busy, busy—far too busy to think about Mitzi. He fills the cream and milk pitchers, and the sugar bowl. He takes out the trash. The Wiltons from room 4 are early risers and Mrs. Wilton helps herself to over half the bacon. She might weigh ninety pounds soaking wet; possibly, she's bulimic. Kelley puts more bacon on the griddle as Isabelle takes the Wiltons' omelette orders. Kelley does dishes.

Jennifer comes down to get breakfast for the boys. The boys love bacon. Kelley puts even more bacon on the griddle. He really prefers sausage mornings.

There's a rush at nine fifteen—three rooms eating at once. Pancakes, omelettes...and the coffee is gone. Kelley brews more coffee. Kevin pops into the kitchen with the baby.

Kelley says, "The coffee is going to be a minute. Do you want me to hold her?"

"I've got her," Kevin says. "You look busy."

But Kelley is never too busy for Genevieve. At four months, she has learned to hold up her head, which is covered with the softest blond fuzz. She has round blue eyes the color of sapphires; Kelley is not exaggerating. Sometimes, in the mornings, he will stand over her crib and whisper, "Wake up and show me the jewels." Genevieve has a tiny rosebud mouth and of course those luscious, satiny-soft baby cheeks. He can't find anything in nature to compare her to except a perfect ripe raspberry, maybe, or a fluffy cumulus cloud. He is *smitten* with this baby. *Everyone* is smitten with this baby. She is, quite possibly, the most beloved baby in all the world.

"Let me take her for a second," Kelley says. "You flip the pancakes."

"I'll mess them up," Kevin warns, but he hands the baby to Kelley and wields the spatula.

"Hello, sweet bug," Kelley says to Genevieve as he dances her around the kitchen. "I'm going to take her out to say hi to the guests."

"I'm going to stay here and screw up the pancakes," Kevin says.

Kelley shows Genevieve off to the couples who are eating; he is a shamelessly proud grandpa. The women all coo and wave and tug on Genevieve's tiny socked feet, but then Kelley notices Mr. Rooney clutching his empty coffee mug, and Kelley heads back to the kitchen.

He can pour coffee with one hand; he has learned, again, how to do everything one-handed so as not to set Genevieve down. Was he this enamored with Bart? He wonders. Bart had been colicky. He screamed all the time, six or seven hours a day, which sent Mitzi into a frazzled state. She tried everything: she set the baby seat on the clothes dryer, she bundled Bart in his snowsuit and drove him around the island, she put him in the swing and the vibrating chair—nothing would stop the kid from screaming. Mitzi read that colicky babies were supposed to be very intelligent and high-functioning as adults, that was fine to know, but it hadn't been particularly helpful in the moment.

Kelley remembers that Mitzi went to the health food store and came home with drops that were supposed to magically cure colic. Mitzi had given Bart the drops—and *sure enough,* he had instantly stopped crying. Kelley had thought, *The holistic approach works!* He had squeezed Mitzi in congratulations as Bart kicked contentedly in the middle of their bed.

"Well," Kelley had said, "I think we've finally found the cure."

No sooner were the words out of his mouth than Bart started screaming again. Mitzi had blamed Kelley; she had said he jinxed them.

When Kelley saw Mitzi the night before, his overwhelming feeling was that he *missed* her. His anger on the one hand and his renewed friendship with Margaret on the other hand—and, of course, his overwhelming anxiety about Bart—had all served to mask Kelley's hurt, his pain, and his sense of failure that Mitzi had left him. She is his *wife*. He *loves* her. He misses all the things they did as a couple: they used to take a canvas bag to the beach, loaded with towels and Mitzi's New Age reading, and they would carry it between them, each holding a strap. They bought matching leather sandals that both Kevin and Ava declared were "the ugliest shoes in the world," and even Kelley had to admit, they were sort of ugly, but their ugliness only accented the beauty of Mitzi's slender ankles and feet. He misses Mitzi's voice when she wakes up in the morning. He misses the nicknames they used to call certain guests—"Mr. Busy Bee Atmosphere," and "High-Maintenance Betty." He misses doing kind things for her—clearing her windshield of snow, bringing her a hot mug of his homemade shrimp bisque—and seeing her face light up. She has, by anyone's standards, a glorious smile.

The night before, as they sat on Bart's bed side by side, Kelley had reached for her hand and both of them had squeezed as though their squeezing alone might bring Bart back safely.

And then, Kelley had offered to drive Mitzi back to the Castle. She was drunk, which wasn't a state he'd seen her in often, and he couldn't just let her walk. When he'd pulled up in front, she said, "You know, I'm not as happy with George as I thought I'd be."

Well, he'd be lying if he said *that* wasn't gratifying to hear. He had been tempted to kiss his wife good night, but he'd refrained. She is only here for the weekend, he reminds himself. Another day and a half at the most. All he has to do is survive.

He cleans up everything from breakfast. There's one room that hasn't come down, which is room 10, Margaret and Drake, so Kelley saves some coffee. He tries not to feel resentful—a gifted surgeon and his ex-wife lounging in bed above his head.

Jennifer and Kevin announce that they're heading into town with Jaime and the baby. Jennifer asks Kelley to check on the older two boys—but when Kelley pokes his head into their room, they are completely absorbed in their video game.

Isabelle starts working on the rooms. Kelley goes down to the laundry to push through the sheets and towels. Ava comes down to check on him. She looks rumpled and distressed.

"How was your caroling party?" Kelley asks.

"Oh," she says. "It was fine." Her tone of voice indicates that it was anything but.

Kelley starts folding the towels, warm from the dryer. "Just fine?" he says.

"Not really fine," she says. "This woman named Roxanne who teaches at the high school broke her ankle on the cobblestones and she was Med-Flighted to Boston and Scott went with her. And he's going to miss the party tonight. So it looks like I'm your date."

"Great!" Kelley says. There had been one second when he'd actually thought of bringing Mitzi as his date. He would like nothing better than to think of George sitting at the hotel alone while Mitzi got all dolled up to go out with Kelley. But going with Ava is a far superior idea.

He can't believe he even considered taking Mitzi.

Except that he misses Mitzi.

But... she's only here for the weekend.

And Ava looks less than thrilled at the prospect of attending the party with her dad.

"Don't look so down," Kelley says. "I dry-cleaned my tux."

"It's not that," Ava says. "I'm just disappointed that Scott isn't coming. This woman isn't even a particularly close friend of his, but she didn't have anyone else to go with her and Scott volunteered."

"Ah," Kelley says.

"And," Ava says.

"And?"

Ava gnaws her lower lip. "I bumped into Nathaniel last night."

"Nathaniel?" Kelley says. "Really? I thought he moved."

"He's building a house on the Vineyard," Ava says. "But he's back."

"Oh," Kelley says. "How was it seeing him?"

"Weird," Ava says. "It was... I don't know... a lot harder than I thought it would be."

Kelley nods. He knows exactly how Ava feels.

The rooms are finished by one thirty. Margaret and Drake have headed into town. Kevin returns from town and the baby goes down for a nap. The inn is quiet except for the piped-in carols: "Away in a Manger," "I Saw Three Ships."

Kelley goes in search of his grandsons and finds all three now plopped in front of the TV with controllers in their hands. The stealing of cars has been replaced by something that looks even more nefarious.

"What is this game called?" Kelley asks.

"Assassin's Creed," Pierce says. "Wanna play, Grandpa?"

A video game about assassination: It's the end of society, he thinks. Then he feels like a grandfather. His own grandfather had thought the Beatles were the end of society—and now Paul McCartney is a knight. He's tempted to run for Coolest Grandpa of the Universe and just sit down and play, but with Patrick in jail what these boys need is a father figure, not a friend to sit down and join them in murder.

"Hey," he says. "I've got some time. What do you say you turn this off and I teach you how to play cribbage?"

"No thanks," Barrett says.

"Come on, guys. You just can't waste the day playing video games."

"We like video games, Grandpa," Jaime says. "Besides, I've already had my non-screen time for the day. I went with Mom into town."

"Pierce?" Kelley says. "Barrett? You two owe me some non-screen time."

The older two boys do not respond. They don't even *blink.* As Kelley is deciding how much of a hard-ass he wants to be, the phone rings at the inn. Kelley has to run down the hall to pick up the landline. He has a feeling it's news about Bart.

"Mr. Quinn?" says a young, unfamiliar male voice.

Bart, Kelley thinks.

"Yes?" Kelley says.

"This is D-Day, the bartender at the Starlight? I have Mrs. Quinn here? She's pretty drunk? I asked if someone could come pick her up and this was the number she gave us."

"Mrs. Quinn?" Kelley says. "We're talking about Mitzi, right?"

"Right."

"And she gave you *this* number?"

"Actually, she gave me your cell number first, which I tried, but nobody answered. Then this number."

"My cell phone?" Kelley says.

"Yes."

Kelley pictures D-Day, the bartender at the Starlight. His real name is Dylan Day; Kelley and Mitzi have known him since he was a kid. Now, of course, he's grown up; he has a beard, a full sleeve of tattoos, and he wears a fedora. He was a few years ahead of Bart at school, and the last time Kelley grabbed a beer at the movies, D-Day had asked about Bart.

"I'll be right there," Kelley says.

"Thanks, Mr. Quinn," D-Day says, with audible relief.

Mitzi is standing on the curb in front of the Starlight bundled in her coat and scarf when Kelley pulls up. D-Day is standing next to her, even though his presence is probably required inside. Both Mitzi and D-Day are smoking.

Smoking? Kelley thinks. What has *happened* to his wife?

He rolls down the window of the used Pathfinder they bought after Bart crashed the LR3 a few years earlier.

"Mitzi," he says.

She throws her cigarette to the ground and squashes it with the heel of her clog, then climbs in the car.

"Thank you, Dylan," Kelley says.

"No prob," D-Day says. "Thinking of you guys."

Kelley bumbles over the cobblestones, takes a right in front of the library, then another right onto Water Street. There are people *everywhere,* crossing the road indiscriminately, swinging their shopping bags. On Main Street, the Victorian carolers are stationed in front of the Blue Beetle, so there's a huge crowd. Kelley has to be careful or they'll soon be singing "Grandma Got Run Over by a Reindeer."

When he is safely on the other side of town—he will have to go out of his way—he says, "Mitzi, what's going on?"

She lets her head fall against the window. "I'm having a hard time."

"You've started smoking?" he asks.

"Yes," she says. "It helps."

Kelley has no idea how intentionally filling her lungs with *tar* can help, but he reserves judgment. He smoked himself back when he worked the futures desk at J.P. Morgan. He smoked a pack a day—only at work, Margaret would not have tolerated him smoking at home—and he remembers how nicotine granted him a few moments of what he now thinks of as fierce focused calm. Maybe it's the same for Mitzi, or maybe she just likes acting out.

"And what's with the middle-of-the-day drinking?" Kelley asks. "Drinking so much that Dylan Day had to call me. That's humiliating, Mitzi, right? We've known Dylan since he was in braces. And why did you have him call *me?* Where's George?"

"George met a woman last night on the Holiday House Tour," Mitzi says. "He took her to lunch today."

"What?" Kelley says, and he laughs. Is George really that much of a player?

"I'm sure it's perfectly innocent," Mitzi says. "But the point is, George needs normal interpersonal relations. He's tired of my anxiety, he's weary of my sadness. He doesn't get it. Bart isn't his son."

"No," Kelley says. "He's not."

"George barely knew Bart. Who was Bart to George but a pesky kid, the one always getting in trouble until you shipped him off."

"Mitzi," Kelley says. It has only taken them three minutes together to get sucked into their same old arguments. "I did not *ship Bart off.* He wanted to go."

Mitzi says, "I know, sorry. That wasn't my point. My point was that George can't relate to my feelings. He's out to lunch with another woman because he's sick of me."

Kelley says, "So you went out drinking?"

"Drinking helps," Mitzi says.

"There has to be something else that helps other than poison," Kelley says.

Mitzi gives him half a smile. "Being with you helps."

She is only here for the weekend, Kelley tells himself. *This isn't permanent. This isn't real.*

Except she is only too real, sitting in the passenger seat next to him, dabbing at her nose with a tissue. She pulls down the visor to look at herself in the mirror, and she fruitlessly tries to tuck her curls under her hat. This tiny gesture pierces Kelley's heart. He doesn't want to love her; he doesn't want to find her attractive—but he's helpless. The entire car now smells like her.

He reaches out and puts his hand on her leg, thinking she'll most definitely rebuff him. But instead, she covers his hand with her hand.

The next thing Kelley knows, he and Mitzi are sneaking in the back door of the inn and hurrying down the hall to Kelley's bedroom—which, for nineteen years, was *their* bedroom. Once the door is closed, Kelley and Mitzi start madly kissing, kissing like they haven't kissed in years and years. Kissing so intensely that they fall back on the bed, and then Mitzi takes off her shirt, and Kelley thinks, *Are we really going to do this?* It's not a good idea, not in any respect, it will only confuse them both when things are so confusing anyway, but he can't seem to tear himself away. He cannot take his hands or his mouth off her.

They make love, fast and furiously, like somehow their lovemaking might be the thing missing, the thing that will save Bart.

Afterward, they both lie on their backs, breathing heavily.

Does he feel better? Physically, yes, definitely! But emotionally? No, not really. He doesn't want a weekend fling with Mitzi, or Margaret, or anyone else. He wants his wife back.

He reaches over and cups her chin. "Did the alcohol cloud your judgment?"

"I only had a few glasses of wine," she says. "But it was on an empty stomach and I was upset about George, and then D-Day asked about Bart and I started to cry. Do you remember when D-Day and Bart were in Little League together and D-Day hit Bart with that pitch?"

"I do, actually, now that you mention it," Kelley says. This is only half a lie. Kelley doesn't remember D-Day throwing the pitch but he does remember Bart getting hit as a ten-year-old. He remembers Mitzi *freaking out* and running onto the diamond and shrieking for an ambulance. Not an ice pack, an ambulance. She has always been that kind of mother. Surely George realizes this? How can George reasonably expect Mitzi to accept that her son has been taken hostage by a force as allegedly brutal as the Bely?

Mitzi buttons her blouse and sits up. "I should go," she says. "I need lunch. I haven't eaten all day."

Kelley swings his feet to the floor. The sex has left him light-headed; it's been a while. "Come to the kitchen," he says. "I'll make you lunch."

"You don't have to," she says.

"I want to," he says.

* * *

It's both comfortable and awkward, having Mitzi back in their kitchen. She leans against the counter with her arms folded across her chest while Kelley makes ham and Swiss sandwiches on Something Natural pumpernickel bread—lettuce and tomato for Kelley, just lettuce for Mitzi, spicy mustard for Kelley, a ludicrous amount of mayo for Mitzi.

He says, "Do you eat potato chips these days?"

"Bring on the potato chips," she says.

"How about some lemon-ginger tea?"

"I'd love some," she says.

He still has the box of tea bags, even though a thousand times this year he has looked at it and thought, *Throw it out. It's Mitzi's tea.*

He puts the kettle on.

"There's something I've been wanting to do all day," he says.

"Oh yeah?" she says. "Something other than what we just did?"

He pulls a pack of cards from the utility drawer. "I've been wanting to play cribbage," he says. "Will you play with me?"

"I'd love to," she says.

AVA

There's a knock at the front door of the inn. It's the delivery man from Flowers on Chestnut with a delectable holiday arrangement: fat red roses, white amaryllis, pine cones, holly berries, and evergreen branches.

"Oh!" Ava says. "Thank you!" She accepts the flowers and checks for a card. Sometimes flowers arrive for guests of the inn, but Ava figures these are probably in honor of Genevieve's baptism.

The card has Ava's name on it.

Scott, of course.

Ava carries the flowers to her bedroom. The more generous thing would be to leave the flowers on the coffee table for everyone at the inn to enjoy, but they're so gorgeous and they have such a deep, rich fir smell that Ava wants them for herself. They're from her boyfriend, the kindest, most thoughtful man in the world, who wanted Ava to know he was thinking of her, despite being at the bedside of Roxanne Oliveria.

The flowers also help banish any lingering thoughts she has about Nathaniel. In the two years of their dating, Nathaniel never once gave Ava flowers—not on her birthday, not on Valentine's Day, not on their anniversary.

Once in her room with the door closed and the flowers placed on her dresser where they are reflected in her mirror, Ava opens the card. Her mirror already holds half a dozen flowers cards from Scott—*Happy one week of dating, Happy Last Day of School, To the most beautiful music teacher in the world, I love you, Ava.*

This card says: *I can't stop thinking about you. Nathaniel.*

Ava falls back onto her bed.

"No way," she says.

MITZI

For an hour or two, she feels like any other living, breathing woman.

It has been so long, nearly a year.

She and Kelley finish their game of cribbage—Kelley wins, as he always does—and Mitzi spins her mug on the table. There's half an inch of cold tea in the bottom; she doesn't want to finish it because she doesn't want the afternoon to end.

"I should go," she says. "George will be wondering where I am."

"Will he?" Kelley asks.

Mitzi checks her cell phone. There aren't any texts from George, no missed calls. Could he still be with that woman? Has Mitzi really been thrown over for a carbon copy of George's ex-wife?

Maybe she has. She finds she doesn't care. Being with Kelley has set her free in a way. She is free from carrying the burden of Bart by herself. Kelley shares it with her. Even though they haven't specifically talked about Mitzi's recurring nightmares—ISIS, the beheadings, the pilot on fire in the cage, her baby boy, their baby boy being the next victim—she feels lighter with Kelley next to her.

"Truthfully?" she says. "I don't want to go back."

Kelley nods slowly. She can see his mind at work, and she knows she's being unfair. Kelley is a man whose feelings she hurt, whose heart she broke, whose pride she wounded. That she is unhappy with George now only means she has received her just deserts.

He says, "Would you be interested in going to the Festival of Trees party at the Whaling Museum with me tonight? Ava has an extra ticket. Scott got caught off-island."

"Oh, I couldn't," Mitzi says.

"Why not?" Kelley says. "We don't have to stay long. We can go, take a gander at the trees, enjoy a few appetizers, and then I'll drop you back off at the hotel."

"I don't have anything to wear," Mitzi says. "I brought a dress for the baptism tomorrow, that's it. And..." She checks the clock. It's quarter after four. "It's too late to go out and get something now."

At that second, there's a trill of famous laughter. Margaret and Drake walk into the kitchen, bringing with them the chill and cheer of a good afternoon spent in town. Drake brandishes a bottle of champagne.

"We've come in search of flutes," Margaret says. "The kind one drinks from." She sees Mitzi and Kelley at the table, and the playing cards scattered about, and her face takes on a composed expression of neutrality. "Hello again, Mitzi."

"Margaret," Mitzi says.

"Hello, Mitzi," Drake says.

Mitzi casts her eyes down. She can't believe what an incredible ass she made of herself the night before; she practically poured herself into Drake's lap.

"Margaret!" Kelley says, in that way he has, as if Margaret is the answer to the world's problems. "I'm going to bring Mitzi to the party at the Whaling Museum tonight as my date. But she's wardrobe-challenged. Do you have anything she might borrow? You two are about the same size."

"You know Margaret," Drake says. "She packs three outfits for every event."

"That I do," Margaret says. She smiles at Mitzi. "Are you sure you want to borrow something of mine? I know that, in the past, you haven't cared for my taste in clothes."

Mitzi knows she deserves this jab—and worse. For a period of eighteen months or so, Mitzi wrote a blog that criticized each and every one of the outfits Margaret wore on the air. It was, by anyone's standards, a stupid and cruel pastime. But it was the only way Mitzi could find to exorcise her mighty envy of this woman.

"I'd love to borrow a dress," Mitzi says. In all honesty, she believes Margaret to have impeccable taste. "And shoes, if you have a spare pair?"

"Ha!" Drake says. "She brought seven pairs of heels."

Margaret swats Drake. "Come to my room," she says. "What size shoe?"

"Seven and a half," Mitzi says.

"Well," Margaret says to Kelley, "at least you're consistent."

Margaret has brought the equivalent of half of Mitzi's closet in Lenox, only far, far more glamorous. Donna Karan, Diane von Furstenberg, Helmut Lang, Roberto Cavalli—every piece Margaret shows to Mitzi makes her swoon a little more than the last. Room 10 has been transformed from the room that Mitzi dutifully cleaned each day—and, incidentally, the room where she had perennially conducted her Christmas affair with George—to something out of one of Mitzi's childhood princess dreams.

Drake pops the champagne and hands both Margaret and Mitzi a flute. Mitzi realizes she is a party crasher here. Certainly Drake and Margaret wanted to drink this bottle of Krug (a champagne so fabulous Mitzi has never actually tasted it) themselves as they made love and then showered and dressed for the party. Instead, Margaret puts on some music—the Vienna Boys Choir—and she and Drake sit in matching armchairs with the champagne like judges on *America's Next Top Model* while Mitzi takes four dresses into the bathroom.

Before she closes the door, she says to Margaret, "Which one were you planning on wearing?"

"Honestly, it doesn't matter," Margaret says. "I'm happy in whatever."

Happy in whatever: this throwaway phrase is Mitzi's life goal. Margaret Quinn is *happy in whatever* because she is filled to the brim with self-confidence and pluck. She has achieved her dreams a hundred times over. She has nothing to prove to anyone. She would look beautiful in a burlap sack because Margaret's beauty comes from within.

How might Mitzi achieve this? She looks into the bathroom mirror at her pinched, pale face. Crowding the shelf beneath the mirror are Margaret's cosmetics: face creams and cleansers, eye pencils and shadows, and half a dozen Chanel lipsticks. But none of these products will help Mitzi. She needs only one thing, and that is to know that Bart is safe. If someone can assure her of that, she will never need another thing. She will exude peace and gratitude all the rest of her days.

Bart Bart Bart Bart Bart.

For a moment, Mitzi is in danger of falling into the usual black pit of despair. She wishes the champagne were tequila.

Atrocities. Burned alive in a cage. Beheaded.

But then, she snaps out of it. Margaret and Drake are waiting. Mitzi puts on the first dress, a luscious amethyst silk slip dress with spaghetti straps and an asymmetrical hem. Margaret has given Mitzi corresponding heels—silver crystal Manolos.

Mitzi puts on the dress and straps on the heels and pins her unruly curls to the top of her head using a silver clip of Margaret's that Mitzi locates among the jars and tubes.

She steps out into the room. Kelley is standing there now, too, with his own glass of the Krug.

He whistles. "Hot damn!" he says.

"That one works," Drake says.

"Mitzi, you look stunning," Margaret says. "Absolutely stunning."

Mitzi feels weepy. But for the first time in a year, they aren't tears of sadness. They are tears of gratitude.

Mitzi tries on the silver brocade sheath, the gold beaded flapper dress, and the white goddess gown.

"Dealer's choice," Kelley says. "You look captivating in all of them."

"Agreed," Drake says.

"Margaret?" Mitzi asks. Margaret's opinion is the only one that matters. Mitzi knows that Margaret lunches with Anna Wintour once a month at the Four Seasons; she has done *60 Minutes* segments with Donatella Versace and Stella McCartney. For the past twenty years—at least before Bart went missing—Mitzi's most toxic emotion was her jealousy of Margaret. But now she understands that jealousy masked her respect of the woman.

"I liked the first one, the purple," Margaret says. "It's a dramatic color, makes a statement. Everyone in the place will be looking at you. Plus . . . it's Dior."

"It is?" Mitzi says. She knows that probably means it costs north of five thousand dollars.

"Designed by John Galliano for me for something, I can't remember what. But I'm thinking it looks far better on you than on me. I'd love to have you wear it."

Mitzi doesn't know how the woman finds it in herself to be so gracious. She's going to strive to emulate Margaret from here on out. She is going to be a better person.

"The purple it is!" Kelley says. He nods toward the hall-way. "Why don't you come change downstairs. That way we can give these two their privacy."

"I don't know how to thank you for this," Mitzi says to Margaret.

"Let's all have fun tonight," Margaret says. "You certainly deserve it."

Mitzi nods. Margaret says, "Why don't I come down at about quarter to six and I'll do your makeup. My stylist, Roger, has taught me a few tricks."

Kelley carries both of their flutes of champagne and leads the way down the back stairs. "Do you need to call George and tell him about your change of plans?"

"George?" she says.

KEVIN

For the first time since Genevieve has been born, they are getting a babysitter.

Isabelle is, quite frankly, a wreck.

She is sitting on the edge of their tightly made bed. Probably the biggest change since Kevin and Isabelle moved in together—other than *fatherhood*—is how neat and tidy and clean and correct his surroundings now are. Isabelle makes their bed first thing every morning; they use the same sumptuous sheets and feather pillows as guests of the inn. Isabelle launders their Turkish cotton towels every fourth day and keeps a big, fluffy stack in a woven basket in their bathroom. Without asking, Kevin has new razors and fresh bars of French-milled soap in the shower; he never runs out of toilet paper. He has turned into a proper adult.

"I don't want to leave her," Isabelle says.

"But you want to go to the party, right?" Kevin says.

Isabelle looks up at him with big eyes. She has just gotten out of the shower and is wrapped in one of the pristinely white towels. Her blond hair is soaking wet, dripping on the duvet.

"Yes?" she says.

"And Ava's friend Shelby is coming to babysit. She's a school librarian, which means she takes care of dozens of children each day. And she's pregnant herself, which means she has a vested interest in doing things by the book. She's a responsible person, Isabelle. Nothing is going to happen to Genevieve."

"I know," Isabelle says, then she says something in French that Kevin doesn't understand.

"Translate, please?" Kevin says.

"I'm going to miss her."

"I'm going to miss her, too," Kevin says. "But we can't take her with us..."

Isabelle opens her mouth—no doubt, she's about to suggest that they *do* bring the baby. Kevin can simply strap the Björn on over his tuxedo. But Kevin stops her. "We aren't bringing her. It's not fair to her, and it's not fair to us. She'll be far happier at home, sleeping in her own crib."

Again, Isabelle says something in French. It's beginning to seem like a passive-aggressive tactic on her part.

"What?" Kevin says.

"I won't be happier," Isabelle says.

"Sure you will," Kevin says. "You need to get out. We need to get out together, as a couple. We agreed on this when we bought the tickets. Right?"

Mumbling, in French.

"Right?" Kevin says.

"Right," Isabelle says, reluctantly.

"Okay," Kevin says, kissing her. "Go get dressed."

AVA

She has waited patiently in her room for her mother to get home, half reading the new young adult novel by Meg Wolitzer that Shelby swears is a five-star experience, and half gazing at her beautiful Christmas flowers. *I can't stop thinking about you.*

Now she can't stop thinking about Nathaniel thinking about her. And thinking about Nathaniel leads to thinking about Scott because of the innate betrayal of thinking of Nathaniel.

She needs her mother.

But when Ava finally hears her mother's voice, it's commingled with other voices. Ava slips out into the hallway and peers around the corner in time to glimpse her mother and Drake and *Mitzi* heading up the main stairs of the inn.

Mitzi??? Something very strange must have transpired. Mitzi is here at the inn. Mitzi is heading upstairs behind Margaret, her sworn enemy.

A few seconds later, Ava sees Kelley follow.

Ava can't even begin to imagine what might be going on with her parents. Their lives are, possibly, more crisscrossed and convoluted than Ava's own.

It's five o'clock—time to shower and get ready. Time to put on the green velvet dress that Scott won't see her in.

Ava doesn't like losing her sense of self like this. She doesn't want to identify herself as Scott's girlfriend or Nathaniel's ex-girlfriend. She wants to think of herself as Ava Quinn.

She heads out to the main room, to play the piano.

She would like to delve into some Schubert or Chopin. Chopin is so technically difficult that it leaves no room to think of anything else. But it's Christmas Stroll and a few guests are enjoying the fire and the holiday decorations. Mr. Wilton is admiring Mitzi's nutcrackers along the mantel. Ava had encouraged her father to leave Mitzi's nutcrackers in storage, along with her Byers' Choice carolers. But her father thought the house would look "naked" without them. Possibly, he knew that Mitzi would be back. *Was* she back? *Back* back? Ava figures that Mitzi has come to Nantucket for Genevieve's baptism. That makes sense, sort of. Ava knows that Kelley and Mitzi still talk on a fairly regular basis—and that no steps have been taken toward a divorce—because Bart is missing. But if there is anything *else* going on between Mitzi and her father, how will Ava feel?

Well, on the one hand, she'll feel alarmed. First, Kelley was married to Margaret for nineteen years, then he was married to Mitzi for twenty-one years.

Then, last Christmas, he was with Margaret.

And now, this Christmas, Mitzi?

On the other hand, Ava has never quite believed Mitzi gone for good. When she ran off with George the Santa Claus, it felt like just one more of Mitzi's phases. Over the years, Mitzi has become consumed with yoga, Pilates, vitamin supplements and juice cleanses, African drumming and healing crystals. The new thing is always the answer to Mitzi's prayers. But really, the answer to Mitzi's prayers—as Ava or any of her siblings can tell you—is Kelley. Ava suspected that Mitzi would tire of George and come home. But is that what's happened? Ava can't quite tell.

At that very moment, Mitzi is up in Margaret's room. But why?

Ava is intrigued, but she can't take on any more drama.

She sits down at the piano and plays "Ding Dong Merrily on High." Ava adores carols that evoke London streets during a new snowfall, the Yule log, brightly lit windows on a square of stately brick homes. Next, she plays "Here We Come A-wassailing," and "Deck the Halls."

She pauses. The Wiltons, and portly Mr. Bernard, who is on the sofa demolishing the bowl of mixed nuts, clap politely.

"How about 'Jingle Bells'?" Mr. Bernard asks.

Ava smiles sweetly. "That's the one song I never learned to play," she says. "So I'll end with 'We Three Kings.'" It's twenty past five; she needs to shower and get dressed. The family is leaving promptly at six. If one doesn't get to the Festival of Trees in a timely fashion, there's a long, cold line at the front door, no place to hang one's coat, and an endless wait at the bar.

She plays "We Three Kings" and tries to sing, though it's really better suited for a man's voice.

Before she finishes, there's a blast of cold air. Ava turns to see the front door to the inn open and someone step in. Ava lifts her hands off the keys. The door slams.

It's George.

George, Ava thinks. So Mitzi didn't come to Nantucket alone! So there is nothing romantic going on between Mitzi and Kelley then, right?

"Ava," George says. "Where's Mitzi?"

"Hey," Mr. Bernard says, "I remember you. George, right? You're the Santa Claus. My wife, Elaine, and I met you a few years ago when we were here at Christmas."

George nods curtly, then turns his attention back to Ava. "Where's Mitzi?"

Something must be wrong with George. Ava has never seen him be rude to anyone, and especially not to someone who recognizes him as Santa. George relishes nothing so much as his own celebrity. He must really want to find Mitzi—and then Ava wonders if he has news about Bart.

Ava nearly says, *Mitzi's upstairs in Mom's room, I think.* But since Ava saw Kelley go up as well, she holds her tongue.

"I'm not sure," Ava says.

"I know she's here," George says, although his tone of voice conveys that he does *not* know if she's here.

"Honestly, George, I'm not sure."

"Would you check with your father, please?" George asks.

Ava ignores this request. "Have you tried calling her?"

"No," George says. "I don't need to call her because I know she's here. I'd like to speak with her in person. Now, will you please check with your father?"

Mr. and Mrs. Wilton and Mr. Bernard are silent, but their attention is fixed on George and Ava, like it's something they're watching on the stage. Ava doesn't want a scene, so she scoots her bench back and smiles at George.

"Sure thing," she says. "I'll be right back."

But when Ava heads down the hallway toward the owner's quarters, George is following right on her heels.

"George," she says. "Please wait in the living room. I can't invite you back here."

"If you think I'm waiting out front, you're nuts, missy," George says. "I intend to find out what Mitzi is up to."

Ava can't *believe* this is happening. She turns around to face George. They are smack in the middle of the hallway, right in front of the door to the nursery, which is closed, meaning the baby is asleep. Ava hears the water running in Kevin and Isabelle's room; one of them is showering. It's time to get ready. Shelby will be there any minute to get her instructions for babysitting.

Ava huffs in frustration and marches down the hall—past the turnoff for Bart's room where the light is on—to her father's room. Ava knocks on the door.

No answer.

"He's not answering," Ava says.

George takes it upon himself to knock again; it's a knock to wake the dead, and Ava winces.

"The baby's sleeping," she says.

At that second, she hears her father's voice. Then Mitzi's voice. Ava squeezes her eyes shut as though she's about to witness a car crash.

George clears his throat, loudly.

Ava fires a warning shot. "Daddy?"

But when Kelley and Mitzi reach the bottom of the stairs and see George, they are both wholly unprepared. Mitzi gasps like George is the Grim Reaper. Mitzi is carrying a deep purple gown in one hand, and a pair of crystal stilettos in the other. All of a sudden, Ava understands what was going on upstairs, and how ill-timed George's visit is.

"Mitzi, let's go," George says.

"My plans have changed," she says. "I'm going to . . ."

"Your *plans* have *changed?*" George booms. His voice, raised to this decibel, is truly terrifying. For an instant, Ava wonders if he's ever hit Mitzi.

Mitzi merely blinks at him. "Lower your voice, George. The baby is sleeping."

He changes to an angry whisper. "What do you mean your *plans have changed?*"

"I'm going to the Festival of Trees party," she says. She holds up the purple dress. "Margaret lent me this to wear. It was designed by John Galliano."

"I don't care if it was designed by John Wilkes Booth," George says. "You're coming back to the hotel with me."

"George," Kelley says, "we have one extra ticket to the party. We thought it would be good for Mitzi to get out and have some fun."

"I know what's good for Mitzi," George says. "She belongs with me."

"Where *were* you all day?" Mitzi asks. "Were you with Mary Rose?"

"I had lunch with Mary Rose, yes," George says. "Then she went shopping and I went on a wild-goose chase looking for you."

"You had dinner last night with Mary Rose and then lunch today with Mary Rose," Mitzi says. "And she looks just like Patti. She and Patti could be identical twins separated at birth. What am I supposed to think?"

"Oh, come on," George says. "Mary Rose is at least thirty pounds lighter than Patti."

Ava winces. She can't believe how badly George is blowing this.

Mitzi says, "Sorry, George. I'm going to the party with Kelley."

"If you go to the party with Kelley . . . ," George says.

Here comes the ultimatum, Ava thinks.

". . . I'll pack your things up at the hotel and leave them for you at the front desk. And don't bother coming back to Lenox."

"Really?" Mitzi says.

"Yes, really," George says.

"So you're allowed to go on a date or two with good old Mary Rose, *that's* not a problem. But I can't enjoy one night of fun with my family."

"Oh, so now they're your *family?*" George says. "You haven't referred to these people as your 'family' all year. You left them without thinking of anyone but yourself."

George has a point, Mitzi thinks.

"I left them for *you,* George," Mitzi says. "Because I had fallen in love with you."

"Well, then," George says, "if you're in love with me, come with me now. Please, Mrs. Claus?"

"I don't like it when you call me that," Mitzi says.

"Okay, George," Kelley says, stepping in. "Why don't you leave. I'll take care of Mitzi tonight."

"I just *bet* you want to take care of her!" George says. He shakes his head. "Are you just going to let yourself bounce back and forth between us like a Ping-Pong ball, Mitzi? I thought you wanted to be with me."

"I don't know what I want," Mitzi says. She looks between Kelley and George. Ava, for one, feels her turmoil. It is possible to have feelings for two people at once, as she has unfortunately learned.

I can't stop thinking about you.

Ava feels like the Ping-Pong ball.

It's absolutely none of her business, but Ava speaks up anyway. She says, "George, I think Mitzi should come with us tonight. She could use a distraction and she's going to look dynamite in that dress."

"No," George says. "No, no, NO!" This is an angry variation on his usual *HO-HO-HO!,* and his last "NO!" is so loud that, a few rooms away, the baby starts to cry.

Kelley leads Mitzi past George into his bedroom and closes the door, leaving George and Ava in the hallway.

Ava says, "I need to go check on the baby."

George says, "What do you expect me to do?"

"I expect you to leave," Ava says.

JENNIFER

She carries a glass of wine to her room, a dressing drink. She takes one Ativan, and then another.

Two Ativan and a glass of wine is like a three-hour vacation on a deserted white sand beach.

She hasn't been out in so long, she's forgotten the routine: long shower, special attention to her hair and makeup. She misses Patrick. He once confided that his favorite part of marriage was getting ready to go out together. They would primp in the master bathroom of their Beacon Hill townhouse, which Jennifer had turned into an Asian-inspired sanctuary with jade green marble, teak accents, and a collection of mismatched Buddhas—stone, brass, ceramic. They played Frank Sinatra and Tony Bennett, music that made them feel like adults in love from another era.

Jennifer and Patrick shared a classic, refined taste. Jennifer had never met a man who was as masculine and sexy as Patrick, yet who appreciated things like the cut crystal vase of hothouse roses that Jennifer liked to keep on her dressing table. Patrick always put on both Jennifer's perfume—applied by running his forefinger along her collarbone—and her heels. The higher the heels were and the more complicated the straps, the more he loved them.

Enough thinking like that. She still had six months until he would be out, and allowed to touch her.

Megan had joked that this was the perfect time for Jennifer to have an affair.

But Jennifer has zero interest in anyone but Patrick. It's as though she punched buttons on a man-making machine, including all the qualities and quirks she wanted—and out he popped.

Jail.

Jennifer sips her wine. Her head starts to spin. She sits on the closed lid of the toilet and thinks to herself, *I'm addicted to pills.* What will she do when the oxy runs out? Fake a back injury? Find a dealer? She is disappointed in herself for succumbing to this predictable crutch. She realizes half the women on Beacon Hill are medicated, but she'd expected more from herself. She should have started yoga, or meditation. She pictures herself on a mat, wearing a cute outfit from lululemon, her body a clean, empty, flexible vessel.

After a few seconds of bemoaning how far she is from that goal, she slips on her new dress, purchased at Erica Wilson that very afternoon. It's black. When she wore black out with Patrick, it felt sexy. Now, it feels funereal.

She spritzes on her own perfume. Sighs. But there is no time for wallowing; she heads downstairs to feed the boys.

When Barrett sees his mother all dressed up, his face darkens. "You're going out?" he says. "Again?"

"I was out for less than two hours last night," Jennifer says. "And that was a favor to your Auntie Ava. You didn't even notice I was gone."

"I *did* notice you were gone," Barrett says. "Because Grandpa came up and gave us a lecture."

"He told us to be nice to you," Pierce says.

"He did?" Jennifer says. She's touched that Kelley spoke up on her behalf, but then she wonders if it's obvious to everyone in her husband's family that the boys are running her off the rails. Do they suspect she's on drugs?

Barrett snarls. "You're all dressed up."

"Yes. Thank you for noticing."

"You look nice, Mom," Jaime says, though his eyes are glued to the TV. He shoots; blood spatters all over the screen.

Jennifer says, "I can order you a pizza from Sophie T's, or I can go downstairs and make you grilled cheese with tomato."

"We had pizza last night," Pierce reminds her. "And grilled cheese with tomato is just pizza in another form."

"How about Thai food?" Jennifer asks.

"How about you're neglecting us?" Barrett says. "Keeping us shut up in this room all weekend and making us eat crappy takeout..."

Jennifer stares Barrett down. "Neglecting you?" she says. "You want to see me neglect you? I'm half tempted to leave you here without anything for dinner!" She's screaming now. Control over her emotions floats away like a balloon. "I *tried* to get you to come to town with me today and you refused! So don't tell me I'm keeping you shut up in here! I couldn't drag you out of here with a team of oxen!"

"Mommy," Jaime says.

"You have no *idea* how difficult it is!" she says.

"What about *us?*" Barrett says. "We're the ones who lost our father!"

Kevin pokes his head in. "Everything okay in here?" he asks. "You do know, guys, that we have an inn-ful of guests."

"Yes, Uncle Kevin," Jennifer snaps. "We do know that."

Kevin says, "It's getting a little loud. I heard you from all the way down the hall."

Great, Jennifer thinks. Now her family squabbles have been overheard by everyone in the building. She should just pack up the kids and go back to Beacon Hill where they can make a scene in the privacy of their own home. But she can't bail on the baptism. She says, "I'm sorry, Kevin. I have to feed these guys something for dinner."

"Isabelle made fried chicken and a big Caesar salad," he says. "It's downstairs in the kitchen. Help yourselves."

Thank you, Isabelle, Jennifer thinks. She doesn't need drugs. All she needs is the support of this wonderful family she married into.

"How does fried chicken sound, guys?" Jennifer asks.

The boys don't respond, but they do set down their controllers and follow Jennifer, their neglectful mother, down to the kitchen.

KELLEY

Since Shelby is holding Genevieve—who seems to be taking to her just fine as long as Isabelle isn't in her direct line of vision—they ask Mr. Bernard to take the pictures. They hand him Ava's phone, Kelley's camera, Kevin's phone, Jennifer's phone, and Margaret's phone.

Mitzi is at Kelley's side, in the manner of a wife. Drake and Margaret are together, Kevin and Isabelle, Ava and Jennifer.

"I'm a seventh wheel," Ava says.

"Eighth wheel," Jennifer says, raising her hand.

The men are all in tuxes. Mitzi is in the purple, Margaret in gold, Jennifer in black, Isabelle in winter white, and Ava in dark green. They are all holding flutes of champagne.

"These are great photos," Mr. Bernard says. "You have a beautiful family."

"Thank you," Kelley says.

"Thank you," Mitzi says.

"Thank you," Margaret says.

Kevin says, "It doesn't feel complete without Patrick and Bart."

"Next year," Margaret says in her broadcasting voice, meant to convey calm and optimism in the face of any Armageddon. "They'll be here with us next year."

Kelley fears that Mitzi or Jennifer might get welled up with emotion. But when all of the photos are taken and the group relaxes, the only person wiping tears from her eyes is Isabelle.

"Isabelle," Kelley says, "what's wrong?"

"She doesn't want to leave the baby," Kevin says.

"Oh!" Margaret says. She gives Isabelle a hug. "It's natural to feel that way. I remember being assigned to a story in

Morocco when Patrick was two and this one"—here, she points to Kevin—"was a baby, just about Genevieve's age. And I had to go for a *week*. The flight to Casablanca lasted seven hours and I cried the whole way."

"True story," Kelley says. "I was there."

"You were working," Margaret says. "Your mother was there."

Drake clears his throat.

Margaret wipes a tear from Isabelle's cheek. "It's just a few hours," she says. "The baby will be fine."

"That's what I told her," Kevin says.

Kelley offers Mitzi an arm. "Shall we go?" he says.

AVA

She's riding to the party with Kevin, Isabelle, and Jennifer. Ava stares out the window at the colorful Christmas streets. Normally, the lights and the trees would make her giddy with little-kid wonder, but right now she feels dateless and alone. She can't because Jennifer is even more alone than Ava is—and for longer.

When they all bundle into the car, Ava says, "Does anyone know if Dad and Mitzi are back together?"

"Don't start," Kevin says. "It's none of our business."

"George had a lunch date with some other woman at the pharmacy," Jennifer says. "It seemed like a date-date."

"Don't *start*," Kevin says. "It's *none* of our business."

"Isn't it?" Ava asks. "He's our father."

Isabelle pipes up from the front seat. "I think Kelley and Mitzi just worry together about Bart."

Kevin says, in a voice that puts an end to the subject, "We all worry about Bart."

Ava decides to call Scott. She wants to hear his voice, and with George showing up out of the blue, she hasn't had a chance.

He picks up on the sixth ring. Since he's left, he has either missed Ava's calls altogether or picked up on the very last ring before voicemail, which bothers Ava. Why is it taking him so long to answer his phone when he keeps it in his front pocket at all times?

Ava doesn't care to speculate.

"Hello?" he says.

"Hey," she says. "We're in the car headed to the party." She lets this sink in for a beat or two. "What are you doing?"

"Well," he says, his voice chipper, "Roxanne is out of surgery, she's awake, and I'm trying to entice her to eat some of this nice vanilla pudding."

Ava doesn't quite know what to do with that sentence. She can only picture Scott positioned at Roxanne's bedside, feeding her. She finds this vision *infuriating*.

He should be *here* with *her*. Not spooning pudding into Roxanne's mouth.

"Please give Roxanne my best wishes," Ava says.

"I will," Scott says. "How was your day?"

"*My* day?" Ava asks. The only thing out of the ordinary— other than the drama with Santa and Mrs. Claus—was that Ava received flowers from Nathaniel. Thinking of the flowers from Nathaniel only serves to make Ava even angrier— because the flowers *should have been from Scott!* But Scott didn't think to send Ava flowers because he was too busy trying to entice Mz. Ohhhhhh to eat her pudding.

For a second, Ava considers telling Scott that Nathaniel sent her flowers.

Should she?

Should she?

She really needed to have that conversation with her mother today. Maybe she could ask Jennifer? But there isn't time; they're almost to the Whaling Museum.

"My day is about to hit its highlight," Ava says. "We're pulling up to the Whaling Museum now. Shall I call you after the party? It might be pretty late. Maybe I'll just see you tomorrow morning?" Ava will have to move the flowers from her room tonight. She'll put them on the coffee table in the living room. She'll bury Nathaniel's card deep in her "Things That Might Have Been" file.

"About tomorrow morning...," Scott says.

Don't say it! Ava thinks.

"...I can't get back tonight. Roxanne is being released tomorrow morning at nine, and she has no way to get back to the island, so I told her I'd drive her back. She'll be on crutches, obviously, and she's never used them before, and..." Here, he lowers his voice. "...I just can't *leave* her here, Ava. She is *completely* helpless."

"You're going to miss the baptism?" Ava says.

"Yes," Scott says. "I might make it to part of the lunch, depending on how late it goes."

It's on the tip of Ava's tongue to say, *Don't bother coming to the lunch, and don't bother calling me ever again!* This debacle is entirely Scott's fault! It was *his* idea to invite Roxanne Oliveria to the Ugly Sweater Caroling party when he saw her at the pool! The party tonight is one thing; it's just a party. They can go together next year, and the year after that. But the baptism is a once-in-a-lifetime Quinn family milestone. The first granddaughter. And Ava is the baby's godmother! They are already short two men with Patrick and Bart gone. Ava can't believe Scott doesn't realize how important his presence is.

However, she knows he's doing the right thing. He can't leave Roxanne to get home to Nantucket on crutches by herself. He just can't. Ava would be disappointed in him if he did.

Deep breath. She needs to be supercool here.

"You're such a hero," Ava says. "Don't worry about me. I have my whole family here to support me. You just get Roxanne home to Nantucket, and if you make it to lunch, so much the better."

She hears Scott breathe a sigh of relief. "What did I do to deserve you?" he asks. "I am missing the whole weekend of fun with you. I know you need me there, and yet you're being so understanding. I feel so lucky to have you, Ava. All I've talked to Roxanne about is how much I love you."

"Well, good," Ava says. Scott's words actually do the trick in setting things right between them. "I love you."

"I'll get home as early as I can tomorrow," Scott says, "and I'll come right to you."

"You do that," Ava says.

Kevin drops Ava, Isabelle, and Jennifer off at the entrance of the Whaling Museum. It's a perfect winter night—crisp and cold, with just a few fat snowflakes starting to drift down. There's a line but it's moving. Everyone is in tuxes and overcoats, gowns and furs. Ava lifts the hem of her green gown, and in a few seconds she's hanging her wrap in the Discovery Room.

The Whaling Museum is all decked out for the holidays. There are greens and velvet bows and white fairy lights—and eighty-two Christmas trees, each decorated in a theme by island businesses and organizations. The fun in the party is to stroll the museum ogling the trees, hitting the bar, and picking up the bite-size offerings from thirty-five Nantucket restaurants. There will be incessant chatting with fellow year-rounders and the summer residents who come back to Nantucket for Stroll weekend. Everyone who is anyone is at the Whaling Museum tonight. The Festival of Trees party is the *ultimate* see-and-be-seen scene.

But there isn't anyone at this party who will be as sought after as Margaret Quinn. She is, of course, a national icon, one of the most recognizable faces in America. Ava knows her mother can handle any crowd with aplomb and that the initial feeding frenzy for Margaret's attention will die down. Ava decides not to wait for her mother, but when she leaves the Discovery Room after hanging her wrap, she realizes she's lost Jennifer and Isabelle.

She'll catch up with everyone later. She knows plenty of people and can make her own way.

She glides over to the bar, minding the hem of her dress. She feels elegant, but that will come to an end if she trips and face-plants.

At the bar, she sees Delta Martin, a woman about ten years older and a hundred million dollars wealthier than Ava.

"Ava," Delta says, "you look just like a Sargent painting. Those shoulders! That bosom! I would kill for peaches-and-cream skin like yours. And that dress is *divine*."

"Thank you," Ava says. Delta Martin has always gone heavy on the ingratiating comments, but Ava has never quite cottoned to the woman—probably because the year before last, Nathaniel was renovating Delta Martin's house and she was forever flirting with him.

"You're not going to believe who I brought tonight as my guest," Delta says. "An old friend of yours!"

"Hey, Ava," a voice at her elbow says. "You look exactly like this girl I dreamt about last night."

Ava turns. Standing behind her, looking way too handsome in a tuxedo with a paisley silk vest, is Nathaniel.

"Me?" she says.
"You," he says.

KEVIN

If he can keep Isabelle happy and occupied for an hour or ninety minutes, he'll consider this night a success. It's going to be challenging, however, because Isabelle isn't drinking and she doesn't know many people here. When she meets strangers, her English flies from her head, and she clams up.

However, Kevin has Jennifer to help. Jennifer suggests that she and Isabelle go sample something from every restaurant and rate them best to worst. Isabelle is especially fond of foie gras and Jennifer of Nantucket bay scallops. The two women lock arms and off they go on their culinary quest. They'll easily be gone an hour. Kevin can get a drink and do some schmoozing. It's been so long since he's been out, his schmoozing muscles are flabby.

Some days he really misses working at the bar. He misses his customers, he misses his domain—grungy though it was—he misses camaraderie. There's nothing like taking care of an infant to isolate a person.

Not that he would change a thing. His phone is in the breast pocket of his tux jacket and he's ready to show anyone who asks his six zillion photos of Genevieve.

He decides to get a Jameson, neat, then call and check in with Shelby. Once he knows for sure that the baby is fed, burped, changed, dressed in her snuggle pj's and read to, he can start to party.

"Hey, Shelby," he says. "How goes it?"

"She's asleep," Shelby says.

"She's asleep," Kevin repeats. *BINGO! Two hours, maybe three!* "Thanks, Shelby, you are a champion."

"That I am," she says.

Kevin takes a swig of his drink, and spins around to see…his…his…*worst nightmare* standing right in front of him. He makes a noise—something between a bark and a bleat. The nightmare has bare white arms that reach out to straighten his bow tie.

"Don't," he says, "touch me."

"Oh come on, Kevvy," she says.

Kevvy. Kevin blinks and shakes his head, trying to make the vision before him disappear. It's Norah Vale, his ex-wife. She is here, somehow, in person, calling him *Kevvy*, the reprehensible diminutive she has always used, even though she knows he hates it.

He despises Norah. She broke his heart and ruined his life. And yet, for one second, something inside of him stirs. She is here, in front of him, in person.

No! He will not allow himself to fall prey to her. He was in her grip—which he can only describe as a Vulcan mind meld—from the day he met her in tenth grade until the day she took all his money and left for Miami twelve years ago.

He used to believe that the snake tattoo winding its way up Norah's arm, and over her shoulder to the collarbone where it lashes out with fangs bared, was sexy and wild—but now he just sees it as a visible sign that Norah is disturbed. It's her calling card, letting the people she meets know she's nuts.

Nuts.

He needs to get away from her. God forbid Isabelle sees her. Isabelle is French, and therefore nonchalant about most things. *C'est la vie.* However, before Kevin and Isabelle were in love, back when they were just friends, Kevin confided the whole long sordid Norah Vale story to Isabelle and quite unfortunately, in retrospect, he uttered the sentence, "A part of me will always be stupidly, irrationally in love with Norah." Isabelle has reminded him at least half a dozen times that he's said this, even as he retracted the statement. "I didn't know what love was until I met *you*." This was met with Isabelle's expression of extreme skepticism.

She would *not* like seeing Kevin talking to Norah Vale—and oh yes, Isabelle *will* recognize Norah immediately. Kevin willingly showed Isabelle *all* his pictures of Norah—from their junior prom to a photo of them drunk as skunks at Sloppy Joe's in Key West, on a trip Kevin had planned as a surprise for Norah when he was desperately trying to save their marriage.

He had caught Isabelle looking through the photos three or four months ago, just after Genevieve was born, when Isabelle was touchy and strange. She had been sitting on their bed, staring at the photographs, quietly weeping. When Kevin saw what she was looking at, he quasi-freaked out. "What are you *doing?*" he'd asked.

"You love her," Isabelle said. "I know you still love her."

"I do *not!*" Kevin had roared. "She means *nothing* to me! You mean *everything!*" He had gently removed the photographs from Isabelle's hands, collected the rest into a pile, and made a great show of ripping them to pieces and throwing them away.

He tries to imagine how he would feel if Isabelle bumped into her first love, Jean-Baptiste, who is now a big executive with Hachette publishing in Paris. Kevin would be pretty upset, and jealous.

He needs to get away from Norah.

And yet—he can't keep from asking what she's doing there.

"What are you doing here?"

When Norah left Nantucket, she swore she would *never return,* despite the fact that she had grown up on the island and her entire screwed-up family lives here.

She says, "I've moved back."

Kevin closes his eyes and thinks, *No.*

"I'm living with my mother," she says. "You heard that Shang died, right?"

"Right," Kevin says. He had read in the paper a while ago that Norah's stepfather died, but he had never liked Shang and so the news registered a big fat *Who cares?* "So that's why you came back?"

"My mother needs help, and my brothers are useless," Norah says.

"Right," Kevin says. He doesn't want to get sucked in any further, although he could certainly contribute a few thoughts about just how useless Norah's five brothers are. He would start with Danko, who had talked Norah into the snake tattoo on her eighteenth birthday. "Do you have a *job?*" He needs to find out, because he can't be running into Norah unexpectedly.

"I'm doing some bookkeeping for..." Norah's voice trails off, and Kevin supposes that's by design. She's not doing bookkeeping for anyone. "I got my associate's degree while I was in Florida."

"You did?" Kevin says. He can't *believe* Norah went back to school. She hated school. And for bookkeeping? She especially hated math. "So wait, how long have you been back, exactly?"

"Two weeks," she says.

Two weeks. Kevin lets this sink in. On the one hand, he can't believe nobody told him Norah was back. His best friend, Pierre, who owns the Bar, where Kevin used to work, would have called him immediately. Right? Was it possible Norah has been here two weeks and she hasn't stopped by the Bar? Maybe she's just staying home, to help her mother. But that doesn't sound like Norah. Norah and her mother, Lorraine, have a troubled relationship. Two weeks is probably hitting Norah's limit. Kevin allows himself a deep, cleansing breath. Norah Vale won't stay on Nantucket, no way. She'll get fed up and she'll leave.

"So, how are you?" Norah asks. "I hear you have a girl-friend. And a baby."

Kevin frowns. "Who told you that?"

Norah shrugs. "Can't recall."

Kevin doesn't want Norah to know anything about his life. She is such an evil person that he can easily imagine her terrorizing Isabelle in the aisles of the Stop & Shop; he can imagine her kidnapping Genevieve in exchange for the millions she has always believed the Quinn family to have.

Norah says, "I saw Jennifer at the liquor store last night. I think I scared her."

"You saw whom?" he says. "Jennifer?"

"I saw Jennifer," Norah says. "I heard Paddy is in jail."

"Stop," Kevin says. He's at *such* a disadvantage here, and every second he stands here, he puts his family harmony in jeopardy. Isabelle can't see him talking to Norah. He has to get away.

"And Bart," Norah says. "Poor Bart! I remember when he was a *baby*."

"Stop!" Kevin says. His voice is too loud; he feels the people in the immediate vicinity grow quiet. What Norah says bothers him because it's true. She has known Bart since he was in diapers.

Kevin has an unfortunate memory of him and Norah babysitting Bart when Bart was ten or eleven months old.

They were drunk and stoned, and they flipped Bart over in his stroller. Bart wasn't hurt, thank God, just scared, but now that Kevin has his own baby, he shudders anew. He wonders how he could ever have been so cavalier with his brother's young life.

"And I heard Mitzi and your dad split," Norah says. "But I just saw them together a few minutes ago, so maybe that information was bad? I figured I'd ask you."

Kevin can't believe Jennifer saw Norah the night before and didn't *tell* him! He had been *completely blindsided*. Some warning would have been very, very helpful.

"No comment," Kevin says. "Listen, I have to go."

"Go where?" Norah asks.

"Go find...people," Kevin says. "My family."

"Your girlfriend?" Norah says. "I'll go with you. I'd like to meet her."

"No," Kevin says. "That isn't going to happen."

"Why not?" Norah says. "Are you ashamed of me?" She links her arm through his. "Let's go find her."

Same old Norah, Kevin thinks, eager to stir things up. She had led him astray so many times and he followed like a little lost lamb. He had first seen Norah in the breezeway of the high school. She had been wearing a black broomstick skirt that touched the ground, a white tank top, and a sequined bolero jacket. Norah had been smoking, and Kevin—brand new to the school, freshly wounded by his parents' divorce—had been hurrying along with his trumpet case, late for class.

"Hey, bugle boy," Norah had said. "Come on over here and play me some taps."

He had barely glanced at her. He registered the cigarette and the goth-meets-vintage-clothing-store look and thought, *Nope. No way.* He didn't even break stride.

What if he had stayed that course, never succumbing to Norah's clear green eyes and that tiny gap between her front teeth? She would just have been Norah Vale, some troubled girl he'd graduated from high school with. He would have saved himself years and years of heartache.

After those first words in the breezeway, Norah had stalked him like a hunter. Later, she admitted it was because she'd heard he was from New York City where his mother was some hot-shot broadcaster. Norah had been born and raised on Nantucket; all she'd ever dreamed of was getting away.

Within six weeks of dating Norah, Kevin had both quit the trumpet and started smoking. He'd also shaved his red hair down to the scalp at Norah's request; she thought it looked too wholesome long, she said. Margaret had cried when Kevin visited her with Norah in tow in New York.

"It's *your* hair," Norah had said. "It's time to stop caring what your mother thinks."

Kevin's grades fell from good to completely mediocre. He got a weekend job at the Bar and as part of his "pay" received a six-pack after his Saturday night shift, which he and Norah would drink on the beach—always one beer for Kevin, and five for Norah. Things were out of whack like that.

He'd barely managed to apply to college, but he was accepted at the University of Michigan only because his mother, an alum, intervened. He married Norah two weeks after their high school graduation and Norah came with him to Ann Arbor. But as much as she claimed she wanted to get off the puny rock that was Nantucket, she didn't like living in the married dorms in what she called "the piss-ant Midwest."

He had lasted one year.

"I need you to leave me alone," Kevin says, extracting her arm from his.

"Leave you alone?" Norah says. "I thought we were friends."

"I'm not sure what gave you that idea," Kevin says. "I've been quite happy without you in my life, and I intend to stay that way."

"Well, I haven't been happy," Norah says. "Not at all."

Kevin shrugs as if to say, *Not my problem.* Naturally, a part of him is gratified that Norah hasn't been happy, and a part of him would like to hear this unhappiness detailed. Probably her relationships all failed and she got fired from a succession of crappy jobs. Probably her car had a faulty transmission or bad brakes and died in the middle of the Everglades. Probably she has been evicted from whatever squalid place she's been living. Kevin has wished all the misfortune in the world on Norah Vale; he has stuck mental pins through her imaginary voodoo doll.

Before Kevin knows what is happening, Norah Vale has her hands on either side of his face and she is planting a juicy kiss on his lips. The kiss is so unexpected and so weirdly familiar that Kevin loses himself in it for a split second before he realizes what he's doing. He puts his hands on Norah's shoulders in order to get her off him without creating a scene or looking like he's roughing her up. Out of the corner of his eye, he catches a glimpse of Isabelle and Jennifer approaching and he thinks, *No! Please, no!* What is this going to look like to Isabelle?

Isabelle gives him a brief look of wide-eyed horror before she turns and disappears into the crowd. Jennifer claps a hand over her mouth.

Kevin says, "Go after her!"

Jennifer either doesn't hear him or doesn't understand.

Kevin turns on Norah. "Get away from me. Leave me alone. You ruin everything!"

The people milling around in Kevin and Norah's vicinity back away. Norah gives Kevin a hideous gap-toothed grin, and then she disappears into the crowd. Jennifer grabs Kevin's arm.

"That was Norah," she says.

"I know it was Norah! She said she *saw* you yesterday! Why didn't you *tell* me?"

"I...I...honestly, Kev, I wasn't a hundred percent sure it was her, and I didn't want to upset you..."

"*Upset* me?" Kevin says. "How about *forewarned is forearmed?* She just *accosted* me out of the blue."

Jennifer gapes at him and Kevin feels badly for raising his voice, but his far larger problem is Isabelle.

"I've got to find Isabelle," he says. "I'm sure she's upset. What did it look like from where you were standing?"

"It looked like you and Norah were kissing," Jennifer says. "It looked *really* bad."

"*We* weren't kissing!" he says. "*She* kissed *me!*"

"Why did you *let* her?" Jennifer asks.

"I didn't *let* her!" Kevin says.

"If I saw Patrick kissing someone like that, he'd be a dead man," Jennifer says.

The words send Kevin into a tailspin. He sets his drink on a ledge and sweeps the crowd for signs of Isabelle. They have been there for twenty minutes and the night is over.

KELLEY

Mitzi asks him not to leave her side, and so they wend and weave their way through the crowd, much as they have in past years. Some people do a double take at the sight of them together, and some—those who are a year behind on their gossip—don't react at all.

Mitzi can't handle any questions about Bart, and so Kelley fields all the inquiries and well-wishes. *We don't have much information, held prisoner somewhere in Afghanistan, thank you for your concern, your prayers are appreciated.*

Kelley tries to focus on the reason they came: admiring the trees, enjoying a couple glasses of wine, tasting the foie gras and the crab salad and Nantucket bay scallop seviche offered by the island's restaurants. There are tiny pulled pork sandwiches on sweet potato rolls at Bartlett's Farm; Kelley devours three.

Mitzi isn't eating at all.

"No appetite," she says.

He can tell this has been a problem for a while. Mitzi has always been slender but now she is dangerously thin. The purple gown leaves Mitzi's back exposed, and Kelley can see the protruding knobs of her spine. Earlier that afternoon, when they were making love, he worried he would snap her in half.

"How about an oyster?" Kelley asks. "Do you think you can eat an oyster?"

Mitzi nods. "I think I can eat an oyster. Maybe even two."

Kelley steers her toward the raw bar.

DRAKE

Walking around with Margaret inside the Nantucket Whaling Museum is slow business. Everyone stops to ... well, for lack of a better word, Drake is going to say *gawk*. Women elbow their husbands in the ribs. *Look, it's Margaret Quinn!* The men stand up straighter and try not to stare.

Some people feel it's appropriate to stop Margaret and either profess their loyal fandom, or tell her how much they loved a particular segment she reported, or comment that she is *even more beautiful in person than she is on TV!* Margaret handles everyone with a smile and kind words of thanks. *How does the woman do it?* Drake wonders. In New York City, she is rarely approached. New Yorkers are too jaded; celebrities are everywhere. Once, while eating at Pearl & Ash in SoHo, Drake and Margaret saw Derek Jeter at the bar and Drake got so excited he asked Margaret if she could introduce him. Margaret said, "He's *eating,* Drake." Drake had thought, *Right, he's eating. Rude to interrupt.* But not ten minutes later, Jeter came up to *Margaret* to say hello, and Drake had gotten his chance to shake number 2's hand.

There are a few people Margaret actually knows—a newscaster from the Boston CBS affiliate, the personal assistant to the secretary of state—and she greets these individuals with joy and pulls on Drake's arm as she introduces him.

"This is my boyfriend," she says. "Dr. Drake Carroll."

Boyfriend. The term actually makes Drake grin. He hasn't been anyone's *boyfriend* since he was sixteen years old. No, scratch that—twenty-three years old, his first year of medical school. Stephanie Klein. He had had to break up with Steph because the workload was too intense and Drake was intent on excelling. And therein ended his long-term relationships with women.

But now he is Margaret Quinn's boyfriend. They are in love.

In love. Margaret shimmers in her gold beaded cocktail dress. She looks like someone from another era—the 1920s perhaps, or the 1950s. She is a Sinatra song, timeless and elegant.

He's in love!

He gently leads Margaret away from her adoring fans to a quiet alcove where whaling ship logs are displayed in glass cases.

"I know this is insanity," Margaret says. "I'm sorry."

Drake takes both of her hands in his. "I don't want to be your boyfriend," he says.

She looks stunned. "You don't?"

"No," Drake says. "I'm too old."

Margaret's cheeks turn pink; it's the classic Margaret Quinn blush that, she once confided, she went to a hypnotist to eradicate because she thought it would harm her chances of getting a network job. "I'm sorry," she says. "I guess I thought . . ."

"Margaret," he says. "I don't want to be your boyfriend. I want to be your husband. Will you marry me?"

AVA

She needs Jennifer, but Jennifer is nowhere to be found. Ava glimpses her mother and Drake, but her mother is surrounded by a wall of people three deep and there will be no breaking through.

Nathaniel is here with Delta Martin. Ava wonders if he knew he was coming last night and simply didn't tell her, or if he called Delta up today and wrangled an invitation so he could surprise Ava. When she saw him, they chatted for two seconds, then Delta seemed eager to whisk Nathaniel away.

There was someone she wanted him to meet who had a potential building project in Madequecham.

Nathaniel had grabbed Ava's arm and quickly whispered in her ear, "Meet me on the widow's walk in thirty minutes."

That had been twenty-two minutes ago. Ava knows this because as soon as Delta and Nathaniel walked away, Ava whipped out her phone to send Scott a text: *I love you.*

Obviously, Ava isn't going up to the widow's walk to meet Nathaniel. She would never do that to Scott. And yet, twenty-two minutes later, Scott hasn't responded to her text. He *always* responds to her texts. He must be all wrapped up in his duties as nursemaid to Roxanne.

Ava stops at the booth for Le Languedoc, where they are serving escargots swimming in garlic butter. Ava loves escargots, but she forgoes taking one because she doesn't want her breath to reek of garlic.

Because she is planning on going to the widow's walk to meet Nathaniel in eight minutes.

She heads to the bar for more wine, and across the room sees Delta Martin by herself eating the foie gras crème brûlée from Dune. If Delta Martin is by herself, Nathaniel must have already gone up.

Wine in hand, Ava enters the elevator. She pushes 3, which takes her to the top floor. When she steps off the elevator, she finds "the door." Behind "the door" is a half flight of stairs that will take her to the widow's walk. She takes off her perilously high Christian Louboutin heels and leaves them at the bottom of the stairs. Ava climbs until she reaches a trapdoor in the ceiling. There will be some clambering required—tricky in her gown, while holding her wine. But at that instant, the trapdoor pops open and Ava sees Nathaniel's face framed by the black velvet sky.

"Hey there!" he says, and he seems as amused as he is happy to see her. "You came!"

Nantucket is renowned for its historic homes that feature "widow's walks," although anyone who works at the Nantucket Historical Association will tell you that "widow" is a modern addendum. Back in the days of whaling voyages, these platforms built on the roofs were simply called "walks." But when Ava sees a "walk," it always brings to mind nineteenth-century women whose husbands, fathers, brothers, or sons went to sea.

The view from the top of the Whaling Museum is spectacular. Ava can see all the way across town to the Unitarian Church, and there is a sweeping vista of the harbor. Lights twinkle along the shoreline in Monomoy, Shimmo, and Shawkemo. Ava feels like she should be able to see Bart, wherever he is. The thought makes her shiver—plus it's chilly and she didn't bring her wrap.

Nathaniel whips off his tux jacket and places it over her shoulders.

He says, "Did you get my flowers?"

"I did. Thank you, they're beautiful. But Nathaniel—"

"Stop," he says. "I don't need any explanations. I know you're promised to Scott."

"I'm not *promised* to Scott," Ava says. "I'm dating Scott. But I'm my own woman."

"Good," Nathaniel says. "Then kiss me."

For a second, Ava resists. She thinks, *No way. I will not do this to Scott. I will not be that person.* But the wine and the beauty of the night conspire against her, as does the fact that Scott isn't here now and won't be here tomorrow in time for the baptism. He's with Roxanne. He has not yet responded to her text: *I love you, too.*

And, it's Nathaniel.

Ava hadn't taken the escargot because she knew this moment was coming. She had been able to feel it—in her blood, in her bones.

She kisses him.

MARGARET

Unflappable is definitely an adjective from Margaret's past.

I want to be your husband. Will you marry me?

She's at a loss for words. The man is dead serious—that much she can see from the earnest look on his face.

Say yes, she thinks. That's the answer from her heart. She is so in love with Drake that every time she blinks, she sees chocolate cake. Lifelong happiness—whether that means fifteen years or thirty—seems like a reality for the first time in a long time. And things are so much *easier* now than they were when she fell in love the first time. Margaret's career is established. She has five to eight more years before she will be replaced by Norah O'Donnell. Maybe she'll head into retirement doing a segment here and there for *60 Minutes*. She knows Drake is on a similar timetable. They'll have plenty of money and time to travel.

So—yes!

But then reason kicks in . . .

She's sixty years old. Marriage means, most likely, moving in together. She is in no way attached to her soulless apartment—a three-bedroom, two-bath affair with a terrace overlooking Central Park. That apartment has a kitchen she never cooks in, a dining room she never eats in. She likes the gym and the lap pool in the building, and she has learned all of the doormen's names. Drake's apartment is much more lived in than Margaret's, but she has stayed there only half a dozen times. He has a very cool platform bed he keeps sheathed in gray jersey sheets. Margaret finds these sheets soft and comforting; it's kind of like sleeping on one of Drake's running T-shirts. He has a quilt on his sofa that his mother made him out of his old neckties. And there are a couple of pieces of good, expensive art picked out for Drake by his friend Nance, a dealer in SoHo, back when Drake decided he should develop an interest in something other than medicine.

Would Margaret move into Drake's apartment, or would Drake bring his sheets and quilt and art to Margaret's apartment? Or would they buy a new place, maybe one of the superluxe apartments in the new high-rise on Park Avenue? Neither of them has time to make these decisions, much less execute a move or go through all the trouble that a new place would entail. Margaret remembers back when she and Kelley moved into the brownstone on East Eighty-eighth Street; Margaret was enthusiastic about renovating it. Back then, she cared about things like stripping flooring down to its original hardwood. She hired a contractor to build a window seat in Ava's bedroom, and Margaret herself had gone to the fabric store to pick out toile for the cushions and matching silk for the pillows.

Now, Margaret doesn't have time to give attention to even the smallest home improvement project.

And what about their bank accounts? Certainly those would remain separate? How would they decide who pays for things? When they go out now, Drake always pays, even though Margaret makes more money. At least, she *thinks* she makes more money. But maybe not. Is it odd that she has absolutely no idea how much money Drake makes? She has never thought to ask. It always seemed like Drake's personal business.

This gets to the heart of Margaret's fears. She has an established life, a certain way of doing things, a daily routine, a weekly routine, a yearly routine. And so does Drake. Does Margaret really want to go through the unwieldy process of melding the two together? Her conversations with Drake now are erudite and elevated. Does she want to devolve into squabbling with him about who should pick up the dry cleaning or whether they should keep a TV in their bedroom? (Margaret would say yes, Drake no.)

She isn't sure how to answer. Accepting a marriage proposal would be so romantic! She loves Drake so much, and nothing elates her more than the thought of heading into her golden years with him by her side.

But a part of her likes things the way they are now. Why mess with perfection?

Drake is watching all these thoughts cross her face—*yes, no, yes, no*—meanwhile, his patience must be wearing thin. But he has to realize that he's caught her by surprise, right? He has to realize that the answer isn't necessarily clear cut.

Margaret's phone rings, which is embarrassing; she'd meant to turn it off before they entered the museum. When she pulls it out of her gold clutch to silence it, she sees the person calling is Darcy, her assistant.

"Oh no," Margaret says.

"What?" Drake says. As a surgeon, Drake understands how potentially devastating one phone call can be. Among so many other things, Margaret appreciates his gravitas, his depth, his steadfast and calm focus.

"It's Darcy," Margaret says.

"You have to answer it," Drake says.

Yes, Margaret has to answer it. Darcy has been trained never to bother Margaret when she's away *except in case of absolute emergency.*

"Hello?" Margaret says.

"Margaret?" Darcy says. Already Margaret can hear the urgency in Darcy's voice. What is she going to say? The U.S. has declared war against North Korea? George Clooney was killed in a plane crash? *Someone* is dead, that much she can assume.

"Talk to me," Margaret says. Drake wisely takes Margaret's wineglass from her hand.

Darcy says, "You received a voicemail here at the studio from Neville Grey."

"What did he say?" Margaret asks. "You listened to it, right? Please tell me you listened to it."

"I listened to it," Darcy says. "It was cryptic and pretty bare bones, but apparently there's news about the missing marines. Bart's platoon?"

"Yes, yes!" Margaret says. "What is it? What's the news?"

"He didn't say," Darcy says. "Or he couldn't say. He said he wasn't able to call your cell or send you an email, he said he was hoping to reach you on a secure landline."

"Oh, for Pete's sake!" Margaret says. "Can I call him back?"

"No," Darcy says. "I tried, but the number was blocked. But it sounded like he really wanted to reach you." She pauses. "I think this might be something real, Margaret."

"Did you call the DoD directly?" Margaret asks. "The number is in my contacts under—"

"Yes," Darcy says. "I called but got nowhere. Kingman's office was quiet on the topic. No change of status, they said. When there is a change of status, the media will be notified, they said."

"So what Neville gave me was a heads-up," Margaret says. "Something is coming in on those marines."

"Yes," Darcy says. "News is coming. Real news."

KEVIN

He has to find Isabelle.

Would she leave the party, or would she run to the ladies' room or a quiet corner to collect herself? Seeing him kissing Norah would have been a shock, but would it have caused Isabelle to go *home?*

Kevin dispatches Jennifer to check the ladies' room, and then Kevin goes sifting through the party. Isabelle is wearing white, which means she will stand out. Kevin had never noticed before how many women wear black to events like these. Norah was, of course, wearing black. Norah always wore black.

It looked like you and Norah were kissing.

Yes, Kevin admits to himself. For one split second, they had been kissing.

He has to find Isabelle. He can't believe Norah Vale torched his night this way. If anything was going to end his evening preemptively it should have been a call from Shelby.

There are couples admiring the trees, there's a harp player, there's a line of folks waiting for the tuna tartare with wasabi crème fraîche from the Pearl. Kevin feels a growing sense of panic. He's not only looking for Isabelle, he's looking for Norah so he can avoid her.

He sees his father and Mitzi talking to Mrs. Gabler, Bart's kindergarten teacher. Kevin tries to do an about-face to avoid them, but Kelley catches sight of Kevin and eagerly waves him over.

Kevin says to his father, "I'm kind of on a mission, Dad."

Kelley doesn't care. "Say hello to Mrs. Gabler," he prompts.

"Good evening, Mrs. Gabler," Kevin says. His father believes in nothing so much as respecting the elderly, and somehow Mrs. Gabler has become the Quinn family favorite. Probably because she put up with Bart's nonsense— although wasn't Mrs. Gabler the one who put Bart's school desk in a refrigerator box so he wouldn't be quite so "social" with his "neighbors"? Kevin doesn't have time to make small talk with Mrs. Gabler, but neither can he bring himself to be rude. "How are you?"

"Now who's this one?" Mrs. Gabler asks. "Is this the one in jail?"

"No, this is Kevin," Kelley says. "The one who has gone to jail is Patrick."

If I were the one in jail, Kevin wonders, *how could I be attending this party?*

Mrs. Gabler tilts her head to indicate she hasn't heard Kelley.

Kelley shouts, "Patrick is the one in jail! My son Patrick!"

The people standing near Kelley pipe down, possibly hoping they might hear more about the Quinn son who went to jail. The other person who heard that loud announcement of her husband's guilt is Jennifer, who shoots Kelley a hurt look, then says to Kevin, "She's not in the ladies' room."

"Crap," Kevin says. Suddenly he knows that she's left. She wouldn't want to stay at a party once she saw Norah Vale here. She would go home to Genevieve.

Kevin bows to Mrs. Gabler. "It was lovely to see you, but my fiancée has gone missing and I have to find her."

Mrs. Gabler turns her attention to Jennifer. "Now who is *this* one?"

As Kevin walks away, he hears Kelley say, "This is Jennifer Quinn, Patrick's wife. Patrick, who is in jail."

Kevin makes his way through the crowd until he's rounding the corner to the lobby. There, by the ticket desk, are his mother and Drake.

His mother looks pale and shaken. She looks exactly how Kevin feels.

"Kevin," she says. "Thank God. I need to tell you something."

"Have you seen Isabelle?" he says. Then he considers Margaret's demeanor. "Have you seen *Norah?*" Norah has always been intimidated by Margaret Quinn—most women are—but is it possible that Norah *confronted* Margaret and gave her the same horrible time she'd given Kevin?

"Norah?" Margaret says. "No, I—"

"Okay," Kevin says. "I've gotta go. I'm going home. I need to find Isabelle."

With that, he bursts out of the front doors of the Nantucket Whaling Museum into the cold, still night.

When he gets to the inn, he finds Mr. Bernard snoring loudly on the sofa in front of the fire. Kevin hurries past him into the owner's quarters. The door to the nursery is closed, which Kevin takes as a good sign. He slows his stride and relaxes a little. Genevieve is asleep; Isabelle is probably in their room. Kevin can't resist the urge to check on his daughter.

Quietly, he cracks open the door. The night-light is on, just as it should be, but something about the room seems off. He checks the crib—no Genevieve. Also, no blanket and no Monsieur Giraffe. Isabelle must have brought Genevieve into their bedroom to nurse. She would have missed Genevieve after being out. But Isabelle doesn't believe in babies in the bed. She likes to nurse Genevieve here, in the rocker.

Kevin looks around the room. The diaper bag is gone. He opens the top drawer of Genevieve's dresser where Isabelle keeps the favorite outfits. The drawer has clothes missing.

Kevin races down the hall to his and Isabelle's room. It's dark—and empty. His heart sinks. He can't call Isabelle. She is, officially, the last person on the planet who doesn't own a cell phone.

Where did she *go?*

Kevin bombs through the house. The kitchen—empty. Upstairs at the inn, the doors to the rooms are all closed, the hallway unoccupied. He races back downstairs to the laundry room—empty. *She's not here,* he thinks. *She left and she took the baby. Where did she* go?

Then, Kevin has an idea. He heads back upstairs to the owner's quarters and runs down the hallway toward the light. Bart's room. All of them in the family have sought sanctuary in Bart's room at one time or another, and Kevin realizes that *this* is where Isabelle has taken Genevieve. He fully expects to find Isabelle sitting on the bed, holding their baby, singing a French lullaby.

But the room is empty.

She's gone.

JENNIFER

She feels responsible for the mess with Kevin and Isabelle. She should have told Kevin that she saw Norah; of course she should have told him! *Forewarned is forearmed.* Jennifer isn't quite sure how Kevin allowed himself to get lassoed into a conversation with Norah. *She accosted me out of the blue.* So, walk away! Jennifer and Isabelle had seen Norah and Kevin *kissing*. Why on earth had he let Norah *kiss* him?

Jennifer gets herself another glass of wine. Kevin has gone in search of Isabelle, Kelley is with Mitzi, and Jennifer has no idea where Ava is; she hasn't seen her all night. Jennifer knows exactly no one else at this party. She should go home and hang out with the boys even if that means watching them play Assassin's Creed, even if that means dealing with Barrett's misplaced anger. But Jennifer doesn't *want* to go home. She enjoys being out of the house, dressed up, among adults.

She wanders aimlessly, studying the trees people have so cleverly decorated: a tree made from stacked books, a tree made of blond wood stacked like Jenga blocks with clear glass ornaments, an old-fashioned tree strung with popcorn and cranberries, and hung with tiny white lights and gold and burgundy balls.

Suddenly Jennifer feels unbearably sad. She will decorate her clients' houses for Christmas right after she gets back to Boston—it will mean a week of twelve-hour days—but she's not going to decorate her own house. Okay, she'll do a little decorating maybe, but she won't go whole hog as she has in years past. How can she, with Patrick locked up? People tell her all year long how they anticipate the day her tree goes up; it is, some say, the best tree in all of Beacon Hill. So maybe she'll decorate the tree after all. It's good advertising for her interior design business. Plus, the boys will expect a tree. Or will they even notice?

Patrick told her last week that the prison has a sad little artificial tree in the common room with blue and red lights. The tree itself is white. *It looks like a Fourth of July tree,* Patrick said.

Patrick would want Jennifer to decorate at home and so she will. And then, on December 23rd, she will take it all down before she and the boys fly to San Francisco to spend Christmas in her mother's showcase Victorian on Nob Hill. Jennifer and Patrick will be three thousand miles apart on Christmas and New Year's. There aren't enough pills in all the world to combat this depressing fact.

When Jennifer rounds the corner toward the front of the museum, she sees Margaret and Drake. She loves being with Margaret and Drake, they are the most interesting people in the world, but it looks like they're in the middle of a very serious, very intimate conversation, and Jennifer decides not to bother them just now. She ducks out the front. She could use some fresh air.

Standing just outside the museum smoking a cigarette by herself is Norah Vale.

Oh come on! Jennifer thinks. *Really?*

She can't turn around. Norah has seen her.

"Jennifer," she says.

"Hey, Norah," Jennifer says.

"I saw Kevin run after his little girlfriend," Norah says. "She's *blond?* Since when does anyone in the Quinn family date blondes?"

"You need to leave Kevin alone, Norah," Jennifer says. "He's happy."

"Wanna know what I hated more than anything, back in the day?" Norah asks. "It was when you told me what to do. Like when you told me to stop dyeing my hair because it made me look cheap."

"Did I tell you that?" Jennifer says. "I don't remember."

Norah sucks on her cigarette. "I got news for you, sister," she says in a voice pinched by holding smoke in her lungs. She exhales. "I am cheap."

"You sound proud of that fact," Jennifer says.

Norah laughs. "You're still as stuck-up as ever."

"Stuck-up?" Jennifer says. "Now there's a term I haven't heard since my Molly Ringwald days."

"*The Breakfast Club*," Norah says. "My favorite movie."

"That's right. You liked Ally Sheedy."

"Good memory," Norah says. "So... how are things with you? Patrick is in the slammer?"

In the slammer. Jennifer wonders how someone as decent and kind as Patrick can be in the slammer while a horror show like Norah Vale walks around free. It doesn't make sense.

"He is," Jennifer says. "He made some bad decisions. So for the record, it's kind of hard to be stuck-up when your husband is in jail."

"Touché," Norah says. She holds the cigarette out to Jennifer. "You want?"

Jennifer has a clear flashback to a summer day years and years earlier. Jennifer and Patrick were on Nantucket for the weekend, staying at the inn; they were preparing a beach picnic. Jennifer had been in the kitchen making potato salad while Norah smoked outside on the deck. Jennifer had plucked two black olives from the jar and opened the screen door. She held the olives out to show Norah. *See these?* Jennifer had said. *These are what your lungs look like.*

No *wonder* Norah hated her! She *had* been stuck-up! In the days before she had children and learned how fallible she was, she *had* thought she was better than Norah.

"No thanks," Jennifer says. "I have other vices these days."

"You?" Norah says.

"Yes, me," Jennifer says. She stares at Norah and wonders... could it hurt to *ask?* Jennifer's desperate, but is she desperate enough to ask Norah Vale, Cautionary Tale, for pills? Jennifer is very low on other options. "You don't, by any chance, know where I can get some oxycodone?"

Norah's laugh explodes like a stick of dynamite. Jennifer jumps. "Oxy*codone?*" Norah says. "Have you got yourself a pill problem?"

Jennifer considers pivoting on her heels and going back inside, but she needs to confess to *someone*. Why not Norah, who hates her anyway? "I do," she says.

Norah's expression softens. "Oh," she says. "I'm sorry to hear that."

Jennifer shrugs. "Do you know where I can get any?"

Norah nods. "Sure."

Jennifer jumps again. "You do?"

"Sure," Norah says. "But it won't be cheap. Thirty dollars a pill."

Thirty dollars a pill? Norah is scamming her.

"I can pay ten dollars a pill," Jennifer says.

"Twenty," Norah says.

"Fifteen," Jennifer says. She *would* pay twenty, she needs them so badly. She wonders if Norah is bluffing, or if she can actually deliver. The latter is too exciting to believe.

"How many do you want?" Norah asks.

"How many can you get?" Jennifer asks.

"Thirty?" Norah says.

Thirty pills. If Jennifer is careful, that might be enough to last her until Patrick gets out.

"Perfect," Jennifer says. "I'll give you four hundred and fifty dollars."

"I can swing by the inn with them tomorrow," Norah says.

"Not the inn, Norah, come on."

Norah stomps out her cigarette on the sidewalk with the

heel of her beat-up Frye boot. Jennifer has the urge to pick up the butt and throw it away properly. She has the urge to tell Norah that those boots need to be replaced and Norah should take the profit from the pill sale right to Neiman Marcus.

No wonder Norah hates her. *Stuck-up. Snobby pop-tart.*

"Where do you want me to meet you, then?" Norah asks.

"How about in the Stop & Shop parking lot at ten?" Jennifer says.

"Ten?" Norah says. "That's early for me. How about eleven?"

Eleven is the time of Genevieve's baptism, but Jennifer isn't about to tell Norah Vale this. "I can't do eleven," Jennifer says. "How about ten thirty?"

"Ten thirty in the Stop & Shop parking lot," Norah says. "I'll see you there."

Jennifer nods. On the one hand, she can't believe she is going to do a drug deal with Norah Vale in the Stop & Shop parking lot; on the other hand, her biggest fear is Norah not showing up with the pills.

She's an addict.

"Do you want my cell phone number?" Jennifer asks. "In case there's a problem?"

"There won't be a problem," Norah says. "I'll see you in the morning."

SUNDAY,
DECEMBER 6

DRAKE

Margaret tells Drake that she can't stay at the party.

"I don't want to see Kelley and Mitzi again tonight if I don't have to," Margaret says. "Kelley will know something is up. He'll see it on my face."

Drake fetches Margaret's coat and they walk back to the inn. Once there, they head straight up to room 10.

She immediately logs on to her laptop. "Nothing," she says. "There's nothing." She dials into her office voicemail and listens to the message herself. She emits a huff of frustration when she hangs up. "It's like a taunt," she says. "He calls to tell me there's news but he doesn't tell me what it is. This is a recurring bad dream particular to journalists. Great source, inside source calling, and . . . the line goes dead."

"How did he *sound?*" Drake asks. "Tone of voice—good news, bad news?"

"The line was staticky," Margaret says. "And it sounded like he was whispering. But if I had to pin it down I'd say he sounded . . . excited. It's nearly a year later and finally they have some news, so of course he's excited." She frowns at Drake. "What could the news be? One of the kids was executed and the Bely are releasing a video? Or . . . the DoD has finally located the kids and they're sending in a team?"

Both sound equally feasible to Drake. He'd like to side

with optimism but the headlines of the past year give him nothing to feel hopeful about.

"We have to wait," he says. "Keep your phone on, by the side of the bed."

"Obviously," Margaret says, "I *can't* tell Kelley."

"That's right," Drake says. "Because there's nothing to tell."

Margaret turns her back to Drake so he can help her with the zipper of her dress. She says, "I haven't forgotten about your question."

He says, "I know you haven't."

They climb into bed and he holds her tightly. He hopes Kelley and Mitzi are having a good time. He thought they looked happy together.

Good news, he thinks as he falls asleep. *Let it be good news.*

AVA

One kiss under the stars; that was all it was. As she climbs into the car with Mitzi and her father after the party, she tells herself it was a kiss good-bye.

Nathaniel had said, *When can I see you again?*

Ava had said, *You can't.*

Nathaniel had said, *How about tomorrow?*

Ava had said, *Genevieve's baptism is tomorrow. I'm the godmother.*

Nathaniel had said, *Will Scott be there?*

Ava had hesitated, then said, *Yes, Scott will be there.*

After Ava gets to her bedroom and takes off the green velvet gown, she texts Scott, *I'm home. I love you.*

There is no response, but then again, it's quite late. Scott is probably fast asleep.

KEVIN

He drives around for over an hour, searching the streets for the red Jeep he bought Isabelle in the spring. License plate M89 K17, oval sticker from the Bar on the back window. He checks every street in town and then he checks the house on Friendship Lane that has the enormous Christmas light display with the big blowup Grinch, the colony of North Pole penguins, the Snoopy Santa climbing the roof, and a train that winds through the entire front yard on a figure-eight track. The Jeep is not in town, and it's not at the Christmas-lights house. Kevin drives by the grocery store, thinking maybe the inn has run out of eggs or cream or coffee. But Isabelle's Jeep isn't in the store parking lot. Kevin drives past the Bar and considers stopping in for a beer to calm his nerves. He sees there's a long line at the door to get in. It's Christmas Stroll weekend; there will be a live band playing. Norah might be there, but Isabelle and Genevieve most definitely will not.

Kevin drives down Hooper Farm Road, which is where Norah's mother's house is—a very plain saltbox with a scrubby, overgrown front yard and a couple of broken-down cars in the driveway, old taxis that Norah's mother and her husband, Shang, used to drive. There are no lights on at the house. Kevin tries not to think how many times he sneaked in through the bulkhead door late at night when he and Norah were in high school.

He bangs his hands against the steering wheel in frustration, and then he drives home to see if Isabelle has returned.

Isabelle isn't at the inn, and Kevin has run out of ideas. She doesn't have any friends with whom she could crash for the night, does she? He can't think of any. And she wouldn't want to be out too late driving around with the baby. Has she gone to a hotel? It's Stroll weekend; certainly, everything is booked. Kevin decides to try the Castle anyway. It's right down the street from the inn; it would be a logical place for Isabelle to go.

Kevin approaches the front desk. There is a tall, dark-skinned gentleman working. His name tag says *Livingston*.

"Good evening, Livingston," Kevin says. "I'm looking for my fiancée. I wonder if she has checked in here? Her name is Isabelle Beaulieu and she would have had an infant with her?"

Livingston is smooth and professional. His facial expression gives nothing away. Maybe Isabelle did check in; maybe she didn't. Kevin knows immediately that Livingston isn't going to tell him. "I'm sorry, I can't provide any personal information about our guests," Livingston says. "You're looking for your fiancée, you say?"

"Yes," Kevin says. He feels vaguely criminal. Why would his fiancée be checking into a hotel without him? Kevin imagines trying to explain to Livingston about Norah Vale. Maybe Livingston has a maleficent witch like Norah in his past?

"Well, I hope you find her," Livingston says. "I'm sorry I can't be of more help."

Kevin holds up a hand. "No worries," he says.

And yet, he has *so many* worries. His fiancée and his baby are missing, and the baptism is a mere twelve hours from now. Kevin needs a beer. He wanders into the restaurant attached to the hotel lobby—and there, at the bar, sitting with the same red-head Kevin saw him with at the pharmacy—is George.

"George?" Kevin says.

George swivels on his barstool and lets out a robust *HO-HO-HO!* George, it appears, is very drunk.

"Kevin, my boy!" he says. "Come have a seat! Mary Rose, this is Mitzi's stepson, Kevin Quinn. Kevin, this lovely creature is Mary Rose Garth."

Kevin smiles politely at the redhead. She has a cosmopolitan in front of her and Kevin, being a longtime bartender, guesses she's from the Midwest. East Coast people stopped ordering cosmos when *Sex and the City* went off the air.

Kevin claps a hand on George's shoulder. Kevin isn't fond of being called *my boy* by anyone, including his own father, but he needs George's help.

"George," he says, "have you seen Isabelle and the baby? Have you seen them here at the hotel?"

"No," George says, "can't say that I have. Of course, I've barely been able to tear my eyes away from Mary Rose."

Mary Rose giggles, then excuses herself for the ladies' room. George stands as she leaves the bar, then he pulls a handkerchief from his back pocket and mops his florid face. "I take it Mitzi is spending the night with your father?"

"Oh jeez," Kevin says, "I really have no idea." If he had to guess, he would say yes. Kelley and Mitzi had looked pretty chummy at the party, pretty *back together,* and if Mitzi isn't here at the hotel with George, then she must be at the inn. Kevin doesn't have time to worry about his parents, however. "Listen, George, if you see Isabelle in the morning or later tonight, would you call me, please?" Kevin scribbles his phone number down on a cocktail napkin. George picks it up and looks at it through his bifocals. He'll never call, Kevin thinks. As soon as Kevin leaves, he'll blow his nose on the napkin.

George takes a second napkin and writes *his* number down. "Why don't you give *me* a call and let me know if Mitzi is staying at the inn tonight."

Kevin takes the napkin. "Will do," he says, though they both know there's no chance the other will follow through.

Kevin passes Mary Rose as he walks out of the restaurant. He nods. She winks at him. "You're a cutie," she whispers.

KELLEY

Kelley's alarm goes off at six o'clock and he groans. He does *not* feel well. Mitzi rolls over and grabs him around the middle. "Hungover?" she says.

"I guess," Kelley says. He had some champagne and a couple of glasses of red wine the night before, but he stayed away from the Jameson. He doesn't feel hungover so much as achy and unwell. He hopes it's not the flu, but if it is the flu, he'd like it to hold off until after the baptism and the luncheon.

"I have to get up," Kelley says. "People want their breakfast."

"Shall I come with you?" Mitzi asks. "Help out?"

Kelley stares at the ceiling. He had been telling himself this was just for the weekend but now it's beginning to seem like Mitzi might be back more permanently. He's not going to lie: He's happy Mitzi is back. She belongs here. She is his *wife*. But is he just going to let her resume her old duties, her former role as wife and innkeeper? He isn't sure what Isabelle will think of this; she's been very quiet this weekend.

"I'm not sure that's a good idea," Kelley says.

"Please?" Mitzi says.

Kelley sighs. "Okay."

Turns out Mitzi is needed in the kitchen because there is no sign of Kevin or Isabelle, which is *highly* unusual. Isabelle is the steadiest, most reliable worker Kelley has ever known. She was back cooking breakfast for guests when Genevieve was only four days old. Maybe she's busy getting Genevieve ready for the baptism?

Kelley makes the coffee and Mitzi looks in the fridge. "Sausage?" she says. "And how about my banana French toast?"

"And some broiled grapefruit?" Kelley says.

"Mmmmmm," Mitzi says.

Kelley is turning sausages on the griddle when Kevin walks into the kitchen. He's still wearing his tuxedo, minus the jacket. His bow tie hangs loose.

"Whoa!" Kelley says. "Rough night?"

Kevin nods. "Isabelle and the baby are gone."

"Gone?" Kelley says.

"Gone," Kevin says.

MARGARET

She wakes up at five thirty in the morning. Honestly, it's a miracle she slept at all. She checks her phone—nothing. Her laptop—nothing. She is anxious to email Neville Grey, but she doesn't want to endanger him or compromise his confidence.

She calls her voicemail and listens to his message again: *I was hoping to reach you on a secure landline...I can't email...There is breaking news on the missing marines...I had really hoped to reach you...*

That's it. It is, essentially, nothing. Worse than nothing!

Margaret shoots Darcy a text: *Have you heard anything?*

She wouldn't dream of texting any other twenty-six-year-old Brooklynite at five thirty on a Sunday morning, but she's grooming Darcy for big things, and texts at any hour of any day are a part of their job. The news doesn't sleep.

Sure enough, Darcy responds within seconds: *Nothing. I've been up most of the night keeping an eye on the AP wire.*

When Margaret gets back to New York tomorrow, she's going to give Darcy a raise, even if it has to come out of her own paycheck.

Keep me posted, Margaret texts.

What time church? Darcy texts.

Eleven o'clock, Margaret texts. *But text me anyway!*

Darcy texts: *You sure?*

Margaret thinks about it. She will *not* check her phone during her granddaughter's baptismal Mass. She texts, *Just send the text and I'll check right afterward.*

You got it, boss, Darcy texts.

Margaret sets her phone on the nightstand and climbs back into bed.

Margaret is awakened by a knock on the door of their room. She hears Kelley's voice. "Margaret!"

Drake raises his eyebrows in concern and Margaret wraps herself in one of the inn's plush bathrobes.

Kelley has seen the news, then. And Margaret slept right through it.

Margaret opens the door. Kelley does *not* look good.

He says, "Isabelle and Genevieve are gone."

"Gone?" Margaret says.

"Gone," he says.

AVA

She hears her phone buzzing early, so early that Ava can't stir to answer it. A little while later, it rings again. She tries to reach for it, but she's too tired.

She hears a commotion in the hallway. Her father, her mother, Kevin. She opens one eye to check the clock. It's not even eight. Why must everyone get up so early? Why must they conduct their conversation right outside Ava's bedroom door? Ava hears the words "Genevieve" and "the Castle." She hears Kelley say, "Mitzi will finish serving breakfast and clean up. I'll go with Kevin to the airport."

Airport? Ava thinks. She wonders if perhaps Isabelle's parents are flying in for the baptism. Ava's understanding is the Beaulieus didn't have the money to travel to America and they were too proud to accept the offer of plane tickets from Margaret and Kelley. They are saving to come to Nantucket when Kevin and Isabelle get married. The wedding has been indefinitely postponed until Patrick is out of jail and Bart arrives safely home.

Bart arrives safely home.

Ava falls back to sleep.

Her phone beeps, a text.

There is a knock on the door.

Really? Ava thinks. She can't rise to answer, she's too tired. She's too tired even to care who it might be so she mumbles, *Come in.*

"Ava."

Ava rolls over. Scott is standing at her bedside, and he does not look happy.

"Hi?" she says. "Are you home?" She reaches for the glass of water by her bed. "I'm an idiot. I can see you're home. How are you, honey? Welcome back."

Scott says, "Don't call me 'honey.' "

His voice is strangled. It is, she understands, a voice filled with fury. *Oh no,* she thinks. *Oh no.*

Scott marches over to Ava's dresser, where he stares at the arrangement of Christmas flowers like it's a pile of dead baby frogs.

Oh no! Ava thinks. She left the card right on her...

"I can't stop thinking about you?" Scott says. *"Nathaniel?"*

She had meant to move the flowers to the living room.

She had meant to bury the card. She thought she had more time.

"Nathaniel sent me flowers," Ava says weakly.

"Yes, I can see that," Scott says. "Do you know why I'm home so early?"

"Because you wanted to be at the baptism?"

"No," Scott says. "Because Luzo called me last night and said he saw you and Nathaniel together up on the widow's walk of the Whaling Museum!"

Ava feels dizzy. She shuts her eyes. Dominic Luzo is Scott's best friend. He's a police officer, and the police station is right across the street from the Whaling Museum. Ava didn't think anyone could have seen her and Nathaniel; apparently she was wrong.

"What were you two doing up there?" Scott asks.

"We were talking," Ava says.

"You couldn't have talked at the party?" Scott says. "You had to go up to the widow's walk?"

Ava has never seen Scott so angry—not when the school committee cut their budget for enrichment assemblies, not when the gifted and talented teacher, Mrs. Fowler, thought it was okay to teach second graders about the human reproductive system. Ava nearly gets her Irish up and fights back. *You have been with Roxanne Oliveria all weekend when you should have been here with me!* But that will sound petty. Ava didn't meet Nathaniel on the museum widow's walk because Scott was gone; she went with Nathaniel because a part of her still loves him.

"I'm sorry," Ava says.

"Sorry for what? I thought you were just talking," Scott says. "Did you *sleep* with him?"

"No," Ava says. "But I kissed him. Just once. It was a . . . kiss good-bye."

"A kiss good-bye?" Scott says. "You said good-bye to him

last Christmas! And what is up with these flowers? He can't stop thinking about you? Does he not realize you're *my* girlfriend?"

"He does realize that," Ava says.

Her phone buzzes again, another text.

Oh no, Ava thinks.

"Is that him?" Scott asks.

"I . . . ?" Ava says. "It's probably Shelby. She and Zack are coming to the—"

"Do you mind if I check?" Scott says.

Ava does mind. She hops out of bed and grabs her phone. Her screen shows two missed calls from Scott and two texts from Nathaniel.

The first text says, *I am still in love with you, Ava Quinn.*

The second says, *Can I please come to the baptism?*

Ava collapses on the bed. "They're from Nathaniel."

"What do they say?" Scott asks.

Lie, Ava thinks. But she is too tired to lie, and she's too confused. She hands the phone to Scott so he can read them himself.

He says, "Well, I can't blame him for still being in love with you."

Tears spring to Ava's eyes. She can handle anything right now except Scott being understanding. She should have told Nathaniel to buzz off on Friday night, but she didn't. She let herself get sucked back into his irresistible vortex, and now she's in the same spot as a year ago—stuck between Nathaniel and Scott.

"Are you going to invite him to the baptism?" Scott asks.

"No," Ava says. "Why would I do that?"

"I don't know," Scott says. "You look like maybe you want him there."

Ava wipes her face. "I don't know what I want."

"This is just great," Scott says. "I leave for a day and a half and somehow *Nathaniel Oscar* takes the opportunity to swoop in and try to steal back my girlfriend." Scott eyeballs the flowers like he might throw them across the room; Ava wouldn't blame him if he did. "And now, you don't know what you want. I thought you wanted me. I thought you wanted *us!*"

"I do," Ava says, though she doesn't sound convincing, even to her own ears. She takes another sip of water. "Did you leave Roxanne in Boston?"

"She was discharged from the hospital at six a.m.," Scott says. "She was happy to get out of there early."

"You did the right thing, going with her," Ava says. "You're a good guy, Scott."

"Maybe too good," Scott says. He walks out of the room, shutting the door firmly behind him, and Ava lets him go.

KEVIN

He and Kelley head to the airport while Margaret and Drake check the ferry docks. Kevin would like more hands on deck, but Jennifer and Ava are still asleep and Mitzi stays at the inn to deal with the guests. Kevin is terrified that Isabelle will try to take Genevieve back to France and once they're gone, they will not be allowed to come back. Isabelle's papers are not in order. It is number one on their list of things to take care of, but they are so busy day in, day out with the inn and the baby that neither of them have time to go to Boston and meet with an immigration lawyer.

Once Isabelle is off the island, how will Kevin ever find her? She has her own credit card; Kevin doesn't even know the number. He can't have the police chase her when she's a grown woman who left of her own volition. Or can he?

In the car on the way to the airport, Kevin tells Kelley about seeing Norah the night before. "I don't know why I talked to her. I should have just walked away."

"Well, you and Norah share quite a lot of history," Kelley says.

"Yeah," Kevin says.

"You grew up together," Kelley says. "I think it's natural that you would have been drawn to her."

"I wasn't *drawn* to her," Kevin says. But he *had* been drawn to her. Isabelle probably saw it written all over Kevin's face—and that was why she left. "I hate Norah."

"Hate is a strong word," Kelley says. "Although she wasn't a great influence. You quit the trumpet, your grades dropped, you started working at the Bar. Your mother wanted to step in and have what would now be called an intervention, but she felt too guilty for staying in New York and I felt too guilty for moving you to Nantucket. And in her own way, Norah made you happy. You were friends. Insepa-rable." Kelley leans back against the seat. "I do *not* feel well."

"You look awful," Kevin says.

"Oh yeah?" Kelley says, perking up. "Well, so do you."

Kevin's phone rings. It's his mother. "They're not at the Hy-Line and they're not at the Steamship," she says. "I got the woman at the Hy-Line to check the passenger list, even. She made an exception because she recognized me."

"Okay," Kevin says. His heart is dying; any minute now, it will stop beating. His baby girl. And Isabelle, the person who changed his life, made it worthwhile. He may have grown up with Norah, but it was Isabelle who finally turned him into a man. "Well, if she's not at the boat, then she must be at the airport."

"Let's hope," Margaret says.

*   *   *

Nantucket Memorial Airport is mobbed with people who have had their Christmas Stroll fun and are now headed back to Boston, New York, and beyond. Kelley and Kevin split up—Kelley goes to the right to check the Crosswinds Restaurant. Kevin heads to the local airline desk, the whole time scanning the crowd. He doesn't *see* Isabelle and Genevieve anywhere. At the Island Air desk, he asks Pamela, the gate agent, if she's seen them. He's known Pamela for over twenty years and the woman cannot keep a secret. She tells Kevin straight out: she hasn't booked Isabelle and the baby on any of her morning flights.

The agent at JetBlue doesn't want to confirm or deny the identity of any of her passengers, but something in Kevin's face must tug at her heartstrings because she does check. No Isabelle Beaulieu.

Kevin checks at the Cape Air desk. The woman working there says she's had three flights leave for Boston and one for Providence already that morning, but unless Kevin has a subpoena, she can't tell him whether Isabelle and Genevieve were passengers.

He has a feeling from the way this woman is looking at him that Isabelle and Genevieve *were* passengers. Isabelle has flown to Boston, which makes sense; if Kevin were trying to get away as expediently as possible, that's what he would have done as well.

Kevin is pacing in front of the Cape Air desk when Kelley approaches. The woman has told Kevin that the next available seat on a flight to Boston isn't until two thirty that afternoon.

Kelley says, "Have you learned anything?"

"My gut tells me she flew to Boston," Kevin says. "Or maybe I'm just overtired. What do I *do,* Dad? Should I fly to Boston this afternoon? But what if I get to Logan and she's not there?"

Kelley checks his watch. "For starters, we need to cancel the baptism. We should let Father Bouchard know, and we should alert everyone else we invited. I'll cancel lunch at the Sea Grille."

At this, Kevin sits down on the floor and starts to cry. He's exhausted and he's still in his blasted tuxedo; he realizes that the people around him must think he's having a nervous breakdown. He doesn't care. Today was supposed to be one of the best days of his life, but instead it's a shipwreck and it's all his fault. Not Norah's fault. It's Kevin's fault. He can't seem to get anything right.

Kelley sits down on the floor next to Kevin and grabs hold of his forearm. "Let's go home for now, son. Maybe Isabelle came to her senses and went back to the inn."

Kevin doesn't have the energy to argue. He'll go home, and if Isabelle isn't there, he'll take the two-thirty flight to Boston. He stands, and helps Kelley to his feet. It's a good father who will get down on the floor with you in your time of need, Kevin thinks. Kelley has always been this kind of dad, setting an excellent example. Kevin wants to be just like him.

In the parking lot, Kelley's phone rings. He checks the display. "Oh, for crying out loud," he says. "It's George. That guy will *not* leave me alone."

"Answer it!" Kevin shouts.

GEORGE

When, at midnight, Mitzi still hasn't returned to their hotel room, George decides to take Mary Rose up on her sweet—if slightly desperate—offer of a "nightcap" in her room. It's beneath him, he feels, to betray Mitzi this way, but this entire weekend has proved to George that he never should have gotten involved with the Quinn family in the first place. For years, he

had served as their Santa Claus, and as Mitzi's once-a-year intimate friend; he should have left it at that. The Quinns are as
crazy as Larry, and George wants nothing more to do with them.

Turns out, Mary Rose *does* have a nice bottle of Johnnie
Walker Black in her room, and she pours two fingers for herself and three fingers for George. They touch glasses.

"Cheers, Big Ears," she says.

This is the last thing George remembers. He wakes up in
his clothes on top of the duvet of Mary Rose's bed while
Mary Rose snores softly under the covers. He sees one of her
bare freckled shoulders and tries to feel enough desire to
wake her up and prove himself.

But he's too old to prove himself; without Viagra, he's a
limp noodle, and he doesn't belong here, anyway. Gently,
quietly, he rises from bed and slithers out the door.

He checks his watch. It's seven o'clock. He wonders if he
will see Mitzi this morning. She will want the dress she
brought for the baptism. Or, maybe she won't. Maybe she'll
borrow a Chanel suit from Margaret.

He's two doors away from his room when he hears a baby
crying. It sounds like the wail of an infant. George stops outside
the door. He waits, listens. He hears the mother murmuring to
the baby. It could be anyone, George thinks. Lots of visitors to
Nantucket have babies. George should move on; he'd like an
hour or two more of sleep, and he could do with some aspirin.

He inches closer to the door. He presses his ear against it.
The words the mother is saying aren't making any sense.

The mother is speaking in French.

George knocks. Then, he chastises himself. Not two minutes earlier, he vowed to be done with the Quinns, and now
here he is, inserting himself squarely in the middle of their
business. But it's exciting, too. George feels like Telly Savalas;
all he needs is a lollipop. *Who loves ya, baby?*

He, George Umbrau, has found the missing persons.

Isabelle, no doubt, checks through the peephole, and she opens the door anyway.

"George," she says. *"Bonjour."*

"Bonjour," George says. He loves the sound of the French language, and he has always loved French women. Isabelle is absolutely stunning, even at this ungodly hour. She's wearing jeans and a pink hooded cashmere sweater and her blond hair is braided. She's holding the baby.

"Kevin is looking for you," George says. "He's very worried."

Isabelle nods once, curtly. *"Oui,"* she says. "I'm sure."

"You two had a fight?" George asks. "An argument?"

Isabelle shrugs.

"You should go home," George says.

Again, Isabelle shrugs. "Why?"

"Kevin loves you," George says. "And you love him. You have a beautiful baby. You can be happy."

Isabelle looks unconvinced.

George says, "Isabelle."

She cocks an eyebrow.

George leans in. "You don't want to end up like us, do you?"

Isabelle gives him a cool stare. But then, she smiles. "No," she says.

"Get your things," George says. "I'll take you home."

MITZI

She's in the kitchen of the inn, doing dishes, thinking how nice it is to be *useful*. This must be how her pen pal, Gayle, feels every day running the doctor's office, too busy to focus all of her psychic energy on her missing son. While she's thinking of pen pals, Mitzi considers checking her email to see if Yasmin has written back with any advice. But Mitzi is slicing bananas, flipping French toast, refilling the syrup pitchers. There is no time for email.

The phone at the inn rings and Mitzi wonders if she should answer it. She decides it's probably fine.

"Winter Street Inn," she says. "Mitzi speaking."

"Mitzi, it's George."

Mitzi sucks in a breath. She would have been wise to let the call go to voicemail. But now is the time to tell him: She isn't going back to Lenox. Her days of being Mrs. Claus are over.

But before she can figure out how to phrase her parting words, George says, "Isabelle and the baby are here at the Castle."

Mitzi gasps. "They *are?*"

"They are," George says. "She was pretty upset, but I talked some sense into her."

"You did?" Mitzi says. "You?"

"Yes, me," George says. He clears his throat. "Seeing as how I located the baby and the mother, I hope I'll still be welcome at the baptism."

"Oh," Mitzi says. "Well..."

"As a friend," George says. "A friend of the family."

Mitzi floods with relief. "Of course," she says.

JENNIFER

She wakes up at nine thirty. She only has one hour to get the boys showered and dressed and fed, and make herself presentable. She needs to think of an excuse so she can step out right as everyone else is leaving for the church, so that she can go meet Norah at the Stop & Shop. What could she possibly need from the store that couldn't just as easily be purchased from the pharmacy downtown?

Batteries, maybe, for the boys' video game controllers? But she's pretty sure Kelley has a closet filled with batteries, light-bulbs, string, Scotch tape, Kleenex, extension cords—anything one might need for practical purposes at an inn.

Some kind of fruit, perhaps? Clementines because the boys like to eat them at the holidays? Or avocados because she's starting a new diet today? Some kind of cleanse?

She decides to tell Ava she has to run a "personal errand," and she'll ask Ava to shepherd the boys from the inn to the church and save Jennifer a seat. Jennifer should make it just before eleven.

She knocks on Ava's bedroom door. Ava doesn't answer.

Kelley and Kevin come busting through the back door. Kevin says, "Is she here? Is she here?"

"In the kitchen!" Mitzi calls out.

Kelley and Kevin disappear. No one notices Jennifer at all.

Jennifer runs upstairs and pops an oxy. There's no way she'll be able to make it through the morning without it. Four left.

She stares at herself in the mirror. The oxy puts an automatic smile on her face.

The second Patrick gets out of jail, Jennifer will be sent to rehab.

She should *not* meet Norah. She should be tough in mind, body, and spirit and give up the pills. She'll indulge in an Ativan holiday every once in a while, when things with Barrett get unbearable. *I wish you were the one who had gone to prison.*

"Boys!" she says, in her Mean Mom voice. All three of them are lumps in the den, where, no doubt, they played Assassin's Creed until two in the morning. Jaime slept on the floor, Pierce in the recliner, Barrett on the sofa. There are three plates of chicken bones on the coffee table. "Get up!"

Barrett moans. *Here it comes,* Jennifer thinks.

"I don't want to go to church," he says. "I don't want to wear a tie. And I don't want to go to stupid lunch. I hate seafood. The smell of it makes me want to puke."

"You like lobster pie," Jaime says.

"Shut up," Barrett says. With Jennifer, he presents the argument for his defense. "Mom, you told me all I had to do was get confirmed...which I *did*...and then all decisions about religion would be up to me."

"Yes, but that doesn't apply here. This is a family baptism. This is your cousin. You will be coming to church and you will come to lunch. I already checked the menu at the Sea Grille. They have a steak sandwich and they have a burger. You'll be fine."

"You said all decisions about religion would be up to me," Barrett says. "I do not want any religion today."

The oxy makes Jennifer invincible. That, perhaps, is its finest quality. For the time that it's running through her blood, she can make the world do her bidding. "You will take showers in order of age and you will get dressed—khakis, shirts, ties, blazers. You will comb your hair. You will smile and shake hands. You will behave like gentlemen. You will do these things in honor of your baby cousin. You will do these things to make your father proud of you. He would do anything to be here himself."

The boys, even Barrett, are somber. Had she gotten through?

"Barrett," she says. "Shower."

"I'm hungry," he says.

"I'll go get your breakfast now and bring it up," she says. She stares him down. "You're welcome."

"Thank you," he says.

* * *

The kitchen is mayhem! Isabelle and the baby are both crying, Kevin is crying and apologizing, Mitzi is cleaning up breakfast and Kelley and George are sitting on stools with cups of coffee.

George? Jennifer thinks. Why is *George* here? Somehow Jennifer thought...? Well, she doesn't know *what* to think about Mitzi and Kelley and George. Jennifer's mother has been a widow for twenty years. She never dates; her life is both full and peaceful without a man. Jennifer appreciates her mother, especially at moments like this.

Kelley says, "Norah Vale was bad news. Beginning, middle, and end."

Jennifer realizes she has walked into the Norah Vale aftermath.

Kevin says to Isabelle, "I thought you were gone forever."

Isabelle wipes her eyes and bounces the baby.

Gone forever? Jennifer thinks. Norah Vale isn't worthy of Isabelle's jealousy, though Jennifer certainly understands it. Seeing Norah Vale out last night was just one of the bumps in the road that most relationships face. It feels bad in the moment, but you talk through it and you are stronger afterward. Jennifer and Patrick have faced several issues like this. The biggest, of course, was Patrick's indictment.

Jennifer feels wise for a moment. She pats Isabelle discreetly on the back.

"Is there anything I can feed the boys?" Jennifer asks.

"Three orders of banana French toast," Mitzi says, "coming right up."

"Make that four orders," George says. "Please."

"Don't you think Norah Vale was bad news?" Kelley asks Jennifer.

"Dad," Kevin says, "please stop saying her name."

Jennifer shrugs; she's not going to judge. Norah is bad news, yes, but all of them, in their own way, are bad news. She, Jennifer Barrett Quinn, is bad news.

She carries the plates of French toast up to the boys and then she hurries out the door, to meet Norah Vale.

Norah is waiting in the parking lot in one of her parents' old taxicabs.

"Get in," Norah says.

"I'm in a tremendous hurry," Jennifer says, but she climbs into the passenger seat nonetheless. The taxi smells like old smoke, newer smoke, and vomit. Norah's mother, Lorraine, was famous for driving drunk kids home from the Chicken Box.

"Here are your pills," Norah says, holding out an actual prescription bottle. "Thirty, I counted them twice."

Jennifer opens her purse. She pulls out four hundred and fifty dollars in cash. "Here you go. Thank you."

"Thank *you*," Norah says. She lights a cigarette, then flashes Jennifer a genuine, gap-toothed smile. "I'm psyched about the money, don't get me wrong, but the real payoff is learning that you're not perfect after all."

KELLEY

He does *not* feel well. He needs to make an appointment with Dr. Field first thing tomorrow, which will most likely result in a physical of the invasive kind, not to mention a slew of overly personal questions.

But for today, Kelley is grateful that things are moving

ahead. George, of all people, found Isabelle at the Castle and somehow he talked sense into her.

Both Mitzi and Kelley are eager to find out what George had said to her.

"Basically," George says, "I told her that jealousy is an emotion that attends very strong feelings of love." George clears his throat. "I also pointed out that she didn't want to end up like us."

"Amen," Kelley says.

Everyone leaves the kitchen to get ready for the baptism—even George. He's going to join them after all, and then he'll return to Lenox alone. As it turns out, Mitzi is *not* just here for the weekend. She is staying. She is staying!

"You know what I want to do right after lunch?" Mitzi asks.

Fix the Christmas letter, Kelley thinks. He'll have to send out another email announcing that he and Mitzi have reunited.

"What?" Kelley asks. He figures she's going to say something about sex, which would be great—if only Kelley were feeling better.

"I want to rearrange the Byers' Choice carolers," she says. "You set them out all wrong."

She's back.

DRAKE

He hasn't set foot in a church other than the hospital chapel, which is ecumenical, since his father died forty-five years earlier. It doesn't seem a great reach to conclude that Drake was so decimated by his father's death and his time in the church so excruciating, that he had never had any desire to return.

He does believe in God, however. He prays in his mind

each working day—right after he's scrubbed in for surgery and right before he's about to take someone else's life into his own hands. He prays for the patient; he prays for himself.

This morning, Drake prays for the Quinn family, one and all. Inside the sanctuary, they present as a strong and lovely group. Kelley, patriarch, is standing tall in his navy suit with Mitzi at his side. And then George, the Santa Claus, sits on the other side of Mitzi, wearing his Christmas tie and a plush red Santa hat. Is such a hat allowed in church? Clearly the ushers didn't speak to him about it; maybe it's allowed on Stroll weekend. Margaret's grandsons snicker and Margaret herself intones, "Oh, George." Drake is puzzled by George's inclusion, but Drake is here, so why not George? The three Quinn boys are nearly identical in their khakis and blazers; they are sitting in a pew with Margaret and Drake. Jennifer is coming imminently; she had something important to do that apparently could not wait, but no one knows what it is.

Margaret says softly to Drake, so that the boys can't hear, "Maybe she's gone to the airport to pick up Patrick. He is the godfather, after all. Maybe he received a furlough for the day. They do it for funerals, so why not baptisms? If you're the child's godfather?" Her tone is so earnest that it pierces Drake's tough armor. She sounds like so many of the mothers he talks to. *After surgery, he'll be cancer-free, right, Dr. Carroll?* Drake promotes optimism—but not false hope—in his line of work, and he won't do it here, either.

He says, "That seems pretty unlikely."

"But how *amazing* would it be if Paddy could be here?" Margaret says. "Just for today."

She is a mother who misses her firstborn.

"It would be amazing," Drake says. But then he sees Jennifer hurrying down the side aisle, alone. She slips into the pew next to Jaime, just before Mass begins.

Drake squeezes Margaret's hand.

Margaret says, "I'm not going to check my phone until after Mass. I'm going to let Kevin and Isabelle have this moment."

"Exactly right," Drake says.

"Because no matter what is happening, there's nothing I can do about it right now," Margaret says.

"Exactly right," Drake says.

At the entrance of the church standing with the priest are Kevin and Isabelle, holding baby Genevieve. And Ava, who is the godmother, and Kevin's best friend, Pierre, who is serving as the proxy for Patrick.

The inside of St. Mary's feels holy to Drake, holier than the hospital chapel which is basically just a tan square room with pews and kneelers. St. Mary's has a pipe organ and soaring stained glass windows. The priest is white-haired and bespectacled and pleasingly resembles Father Dennis, the priest of Drake's youth.

The priest raises his hands in the air and announces to the church that a new member is about to join their community of faith, and that this member is named Genevieve Helene Quinn.

Margaret sniffs. Drake feels a wave of love so intense it nearly bowls him over.

AVA

There is a long moment while they're waiting in the front vestibule of the church when Ava gets to hold baby Genevieve. She is wearing a long white gown and a cap that frames her beautiful blue-eyed face. Ava isn't overly religious—none of the Quinns are—but Ava plans on taking her role as godmother *very* seriously. She is Genevieve's spiritual adviser, someone to talk to when Genevieve doesn't want to talk to her parents.

Ava strokes the baby's cheek. She gazes up at Ava with her sapphire eyes while Ava tells her, *The most important thing is that you grow up strong. You will be* your own person, *with your own interests and values and talents. You don't need a man to define you!*

Ava thinks this last phrase with no small amount of vigor.

Scott isn't here. And Nathaniel isn't here. Ava is happy about this! She's glad! She is not a baton to be handed back and forth between them, nor a prize to be won. She is her own person. She is, among so many other things, the godmother of this beautiful baby.

It is only in processing down the aisle that Ava sees Scott. He's impossible to miss—tall and broad-shouldered, sitting a pew behind Margaret and Drake and the boys, two pews behind Mitzi and Kelley and George. So much for "being her own person"—Ava's heart swells, and her eyes sting with tears of gratitude. He came! Despite Ava's reprehensible behavior this weekend, he came to the baptism. She wants to reach out and touch his shoulder as she passes, but then she remembers that she's the godmother. She needs to focus on the altar, and the task at hand.

Baby Genevieve is prayed over and anointed with the oil of chrism. Kevin and Isabelle vow to raise Genevieve in the Catholic faith. Ava and Pierre-as-proxy agree to serve as the child's godparents. The congregation agrees to participate in raising Genevieve as a member of their spiritual community. Then, Genevieve is sprinkled with holy water, and she doesn't make a single peep. She just blinks and wrinkles her nose as the water drips off her forehead. The congregation utter oohs and ahhs as Genevieve is presented; everyone applauds. Then, it is time to resume Mass—offering, hymns, the liturgy.

Ava sees Nathaniel as he approaches the altar for communion. She blinks. Nathaniel. As he passes by her pew, he winks at her. She feels herself blush.

She gazes over at baby Genevieve, who is now asleep in Kevin's arms, and thinks, *I really don't have any words of advice at all.* The world is an endlessly confounding place.

MARGARET

Unflappable has never applied to Margaret when she's been at church, and especially not when the communion hymn is "I Am the Bread of Life," as it is today. This song *always* makes Margaret cry. *And I will raise you up...and I will raise you up, and I will ra-aise you up on the last day.*

Drake offers Margaret his handkerchief and Margaret dabs at her eyes.

She leans over to him and whispers in his ear. "Yes."

"Yes, what?" he whispers back.

"Yes, I will be your wife," she says.

AVA

As the godmother, Ava has to be in all the photographs after the service. She had thought Scott might leave, but he sticks around, sitting in his pew until they've run the gamut from just Kevin and Isabelle and Genevieve to the entire family—meaning Mitzi, but not George, Margaret, but not Drake.

"Drake should be in the pictures," Margaret says in Ava's ear. "We're getting married."

"You *are?*" Ava whispers back.

"Sssshhh," Margaret says. "Don't tell anyone just yet. This is Kevin's moment."

Ava nods and smiles dutifully for the camera. Her mother is going to marry Drake. They are going to be *very happy*— Ava can feel it in her bones. She doesn't understand how she can be so sure about her mother's romantic prospects and so unsure about her own.

After pictures, Ava approaches Scott. "Are you coming to lunch?" she asks.

"No," he says. "I don't think so."

Ava stammers. "Oh...okay?" She had thought that him showing up to the service and sitting through pictures meant that she was forgiven. She had thought they would pick up where they left off at their last happy moment—singing carols in their hideous sweaters at Our Island Home. She had thought Scott might make a joke about introducing Nathaniel to Roxanne, at which point, Ava would say, *Nathaniel is thirty-two, isn't that a little old for Roxanne?*

Scott says, "I'm going to give you some space for a while. Let you figure out what you want."

"It's like you said this morning," Ava says. "I want you. I want us. I want to get married and have a baby." She points to Shelby and Zack, who are leaving the church hand in hand. "I want *that.*"

"I know you want to get married and have children," Scott says. "But maybe not with me."

Ava opens her mouth and no words come out. She doesn't want to make a scene. They are still in the sanctuary, and Ava's family is milling about. Jennifer is over by the candles with Barrett; her voice is probably louder than it ought to be as she speaks to Barrett about his "piss-poor attitude" since his father has been gone. Thankfully, Kelley shuttles Jennifer and Barrett out the door.

Scott says, "Ava, I'm tired. I've barely slept in two days, and I have to pick up Roxanne's prescriptions at the pharmacy and drop them off at her house."

"What?" Ava says. Roxanne, again! She wonders if Scott's offer of "space" doesn't have something to do with Roxanne. Maybe during the past thirty-six hours, he has fallen a little in love with Mz. Ohhhhhh.

"Ava," Scott says wearily. "I'll talk to you later."

"When later?" she says.

"I don't know," Scott says. "I'm sure I'll see you tomorrow at school."

Naturally, Ava *will* see Scott tomorrow at school—and the next day, and the day after that. How awkward it will be to see Scott in his capacity *as her boss* while their relationship is suspended, while he is, ostensibly, *giving her space.* How are they supposed to work in the same building? What will she say to him when they're standing next to each other in line at the cafeteria?

"You can't give me space," Ava says.

"You need it," Scott says. He kisses her gently on the lips, and it feels exactly like a kiss good-bye.

Ava watches Scott stride out of the church. She wonders how she could have so thoroughly dismantled her relationship over the course of one short weekend.

She takes a deep breath and reacquaints herself with her purse and her wrap. Now, everyone else has left the church and will be on their way to the Sea Grille for lunch, leaving Ava stranded. Certainly the rest of her family assumed she was getting a ride to the restaurant with Scott. She'll have to walk all the way back to the inn and get her own car.

When she steps out of the church into the glare of the bright, cold day, she sees Nathaniel on the sidewalk waiting for her.

She shakes her head. This isn't happening! For two and a half years, she couldn't get the guy to pay attention to her—now, he won't leave her alone! Now, he has effectively ravaged the great thing Ava had going with Scott. Scott must have seen Nathaniel when he left the church. Possibly, Scott thought Ava had asked Nathaniel to linger after the service.

She says, "Honestly? You can't stay away? You can't leave me alone? Scott just basically *broke up with me*— because of you! Because he thinks I'm 'confused' and 'need space'! And you know what? I *am* confused!" She's on the verge of tears. Her Christmas Stroll weekend is ruined. Nothing turned out the way it was supposed to. Her caroling party was a disaster, the Festival of Trees a catastrophe, and now here she is, godmother to the most precious baby girl in all the world and she's about to weep on the front steps of the church.

"Ava," Nathaniel says, "I'm not giving up. I'm not going away. I love you."

He loves her.

She's going to have to make a decision.

Nathaniel says, "What are you doing right now? Do you want to go for a ride up the beach? Do you want to go to my house and watch the Patriots? I'll make my white chicken chili."

"I'm going to lunch with my family," Ava says. "They all left without me."

"Do you want me to come with you?" Nathaniel asks. "Or can I give you a ride?"

"No thank you," Ava says. "I'm going alone."

MARGARET

Margaret and Drake ride from the church to the Sea Grille with Mitzi and Kelley. As soon as Margaret is ensconced in the backseat, she whips out her phone.

Somehow, Kelley sees her. "Always working, Margaret."

Margaret is so tense, she nearly snaps at him. This used to be Kelley's refrain with her throughout the entirety of their marriage, which ended twenty years ago—so why does Margaret still have to listen to it? Margaret is only "working" because it involves Kelley's son!

"That's right," she murmurs.

Mitzi swats Kelley on the arm. "She has a very important job."

"I know, I know," Kelley says.

Margaret can feel Drake's gaze on her.

There are no texts, no calls, no emails. And no new headlines on the CBS website.

Slowly, Margaret shakes her head.

KEVIN

From the instant he walks into the Sea Grille for lunch, he can tell it's going to be a disappointment. Or maybe he's just tired. Isabelle is fretting because the baby is having a meltdown.

Kevin says, "She was a perfect angel at church. That's the important thing."

Isabelle says, "She needs her nap, Kevin. She did not sleep well last night." There is an accusatory tone to

Isabelle's voice, and Kevin almost takes the bait. He almost says, *And whose fault is* that? *Who took the baby to sleep in an* unfamiliar room *at a* strange hotel? But he holds his tongue. He has apologized for his conversation with Norah Vale; he has reassured Isabelle that Norah is *rien,* nothing, while Isabelle is *tout,* everything. They have kissed and made up. He doesn't want to revisit the topic.

He says, "We'll put her down for a nap right after lunch."

Isabelle nods, tight-lipped. They carry Genevieve, who is now screaming bloody murder, into the restaurant.

Kelley and Mitzi are already at the table. When Kevin said earlier that Kelley looked awful, he meant it. His father's skin is gray; he looks like a pencil drawing of his usual self, and his hands shake as he brings a glass of ice water to his lips. Next to Kelley, Mitzi is smiling, but skeletal; she has lost a lot of weight over the past year.

Both Kelley and Mitzi swivel in their chairs as soon as they hear the baby. Kevin wouldn't be surprised if the whole island can hear the baby. Genevieve is howling so loudly, her car seat vibrates. Her tiny mouth is wide open and Kevin can see clear down her throat.

Mitzi stands up. "Oh, poor little thing. Can I hold her?"

Kevin feels Isabelle stiffen next to him. The rest of the family has rolled along pretty easily with Mitzi's apparent return to the homestead, but Isabelle remains nonplussed. *Mitzi is* back? she asked incredulously on Saturday night, before they all went out. *She is* forgiven? She had asked Kevin who made breakfast in her absence, and when Kevin said, "Mitzi did," Isabelle emitted a high-pitched, very unhappy *Ha!*

Reluctantly, Isabelle hands the baby over to Mitzi. Mitzi says, "Oh, sweetheart, peanut, look at you. You are such a darling, yummy baby, just like your Uncle Bart used to be."

Somehow Genevieve stops crying for a second. She studies the unfamiliar face and voice of the woman who is now holding her. Then, she starts crying again—louder now, if that's even possible.

Kelley says, "I'll hold her."

Mitzi says, "I thought she'd like me. Babies usually like me."

"It has nothing to do with like or not like," Kevin says. "She's tired."

"She needs a nap," Isabelle says.

Kevin really wants to get this lunch moving along, but to do so, he needs the rest of his family. Where *is* everyone?

Margaret and Drake enter next. Margaret makes a beeline for the table with her scarf covering most of her face, her sunglasses on, and her head bent, but still a murmur rolls through the restaurant like a wave. *Margaret Quinn.*

Margaret reaches for the baby. "Come to Mimi."

Kelley takes the baby from Mitzi and hands her to Margaret. The baby howls.

Mitzi says, "She won't stop crying for Margaret either."

Margaret seems to take this as a challenge. She flips Genevieve into the "football hold." Genevieve is facing the ground while Margaret's arms support her lengthwise. "This used to work with Kevin," she says.

Still, Genevieve screams. Kevin takes a seat at the head of the table; he feels like the ruler of a revolting nation. Isabelle sits next to Kevin, even though Kevin can tell all she wants to do is grab Genevieve and take her back to the inn for a nap.

Why did they ever think this lunch would be a good idea?

He flags a waiter. "Can you bring us some bread, please?" he asks. "And I'd love a beer."

"Glass of chardonnay," Mitzi says.

"Make that two," Margaret says. She looks at Kevin. "Should I take her outside?"

"It's too cold outside, Mom," Kevin says. He turns to face the door. He needs Ava, Jennifer, and the boys to show up, pronto!

"Here," Drake says, "let me hold her."

Margaret hands Genevieve to Drake. This is getting absurd, Kevin thinks. It's a game of Hot Potato. The only person who hasn't held the baby is their waiter. But Genevieve calms down in Drake's arms; he's rubbing the base of her scalp with two fingers.

"The baby whisperer," Margaret says.

Drake operates on babies; he probably has more experience with infants than all of the rest of them put together. Once Genevieve is sucking in raggedy breaths, Drake lowers her into Isabelle's arms.

Ahhhhhh. Everyone at the table visibly relaxes.

Margaret says, "I don't want to distract from my granddaughter's big day, but I have an announcement to make. I'll tell you and then you can forget about it for a while."

"Nice setup," Kevin says. "What is it?"

"Drake and I are getting married."

Kelley stands up to shake Drake's hand. "Welcome to the family, Dr. Carroll. I heartily approve."

"Well, it's always good to get approval from the ex-husband," Drake says, grinning.

"That's wonderful news!" Mitzi says. "Congratulations!"

"Thank you," Margaret says. "It *is* wonderful news. Just please don't tell anyone yet. I don't want to see it on Page Six tomorrow morning. I'll let my publicist know when I get back to New York."

"I'm happy for you, Mom," Kevin says. Their drinks arrive along with two baskets of warm rolls, scones, and crisp, delicate grissini. Kevin downs half his beer instantly and takes a giant bite of a cheesy scone. He's *starving*. He has a toast prepared, but he wants to wait until everyone else arrives.

They sit in an increasingly awkward silence as they wait for Ava, Jennifer, and the boys. There are two extra seats at the table, meant symbolically for Patrick and Bart. This was Kevin's idea. He misses his brothers. His whole life he has been defined by being squeezed between them. He had thought that with them gone, he might change into a different kind of person, but as it turns out, he's exactly the same. He's a lover, not a fighter, he wants peace more than money, and his greatest dream is a family of his own.

Kevin hears Jennifer before he sees her. She is shouting at Barrett, and when Kevin turns around, she's pulling Barrett toward the table by the sleeve of his blazer.

"It does *not* smell funny in here," Jennifer says. "You will sit and eat with our family."

"*There* are my handsome grandsons," Margaret says diplomatically.

Pierce and Jaime take seats at the table without fanfare; Pierce even puts his napkin on his lap.

"This isn't *our* family," Barrett says. "This is *Dad's* family, and Dad's not even *here*."

Kelley stands up and takes Barrett by the arm. "Outside," he says. "Now."

"But Grandpa," Barrett says.

"Now," Kelley says.

Jennifer collapses in a chair. "Chardonnay, please," she says to the waiter. She drops her head in her hands. "I've had it with that kid. I have ... *had* it."

"I was worse when I was that age," Kevin says. "I promise you."

Jennifer tousles Jaime's hair. He wriggles under her hand

and excuses himself for the bathroom. Pierce gets up to follow him, and Jennifer says, "Not both of you at once."

"But I have to go, *too,*" Pierce says.

"Fine!" Jennifer says. "Go, then!" She turns back to the
adults. "It's just so hard doing everything by myself. For the
past year, I've been their mother *and* their father. And I'm
trying to build my business and generate income, in case
Patrick doesn't get hired right away when he gets out. It's
exhausting." She looks at Kevin, Kelley, Margaret. "I need
help. Can't you people see that I need *help?* I know the kids
play too many video games. I know they should be outside
throwing the lacrosse ball, or I should be teaching them
cribbage. I know I should be reading to Jaime at night. I read
all seven *Harry Potter* books to Barrett and all three *Hunger
Games* books to Pierce. The youngest always gets short
shrift and it's not fair. Is it any wonder he crawls into bed
with me every night? He needs my attention and the only
time he can get it is when I'm asleep." Jennifer points at
Genevieve, asleep in Isabelle's arms. "I want *that* back. I
want the cooing, the gummy smiles. I want them before they
learn how to talk. I want them before they start to hate me."

"Jennifer," Margaret says, "they do *not* hate you."

"Barrett does," Jennifer says. "He wishes I had gone to
jail instead of Patrick…"

"No," Mitzi says.

"His words, verbatim," Jennifer says. "And you know
what I told Barrett? I told him that I would *never* be the one
to go to jail because I would never, *ever* have made the
thoughtless, morally corrupt choices that his father made."

Whoa. Kevin—and everyone else at the table—sit in a
stunned silence. Even Margaret, the woman who has a
silver-tongued response for everything, is staring at Jennifer
in a horrified stupor. Part of the surprise is how uncharacter-

istic this outburst is coming from Jennifer. The woman is so cool, so together. Kevin has always thought Patrick was lucky to have found Jennifer, but never more so than this past year when Jennifer stood by her man and somehow managed to keep their domestic life intact. She took the boys to lacrosse practice, she made chicken pot pie from scratch.

Jennifer's voice is too loud for the restaurant. Tables around them have quieted and are, no doubt, listening in on the Quinn family drama. The waiter, perhaps thinking that Jennifer is complaining about the service, brings Jennifer's wine and gives menus to everyone at the table.

Kevin says, "Can we get two orders of calamari right away? And some potato skins for the boys."

The waiter nods, then gets the heck out of there.

Margaret says, "You're right, Jennifer, you're right. Patrick's actions were shortsighted and greedy. He has done you and the boys a great disservice."

Whoa again, Kevin thinks. In thirty-seven years, Kevin has never heard Margaret say a negative word about Patrick. Okay, that's probably hyperbole. But it's pretty well documented that Patrick is Margaret's favorite, even if she would never admit it. He's probably Kelley's favorite as well. The firstborn son, the heir to the Quinn family throne, the golden child.

Kevin isn't pleased that the conversation has turned to Patrick on the day of Genevieve's christening. And, he hasn't forgotten, he's angry at Jennifer for not giving him the heads-up about Norah!

Where on *earth* is Ava? Kevin wonders.

Kelley returns to the table with a seemingly chastened Barrett.

"Sorry, Mom," Barrett mumbles.

Jennifer mops her face with a napkin. She has *completely* lost her composure. It's almost as if it isn't Jennifer Barrett

Quinn at the table, but rather her doppelgänger, or a Jennifer who has been body-snatched and replaced by an alien.

Is she *on* something? Kevin wonders.

"Wow," Kelley says. "You all look totally miserable. What did I miss?"

"Can we order?" Kevin asks. "Please?"

Pierce and Jaime return to their seats. Pierce is holding a sprig of mistletoe he must have stolen from somewhere in the restaurant. He holds it over his mother's head and gives her a kiss. This gets a smile out of her.

"I think I'll have the lobster bisque," Drake says.

"Does anyone remember the time...," Kelley says.

"Yes, Dad," Kevin says. *Quinn Family Legend,* he thinks: *the Sea Grille edition.* Kelley once ordered the lobster bisque, which comes covered with a dill puff pastry. When Kelley poked through the puff pastry, there was no soup in the bowl.

They have to mention it every time they eat at the Sea Grille. The story is tired, but it's preferable to discussing Patrick's character flaws and the way he's let them all down.

Kevin stands up, his near-empty beer in hand. "I'm not going to wait for Ava," he says. "I'd like to make a toast." He checks around the table to make sure all eyes are on him: Mitzi and Kelley, check, Margaret and Drake, check, Barrett, check, Jaime is picking the berries off the mistletoe and trying to sink them in his water glass, Jennifer is drinking her wine, Pierce is looking at something under the table, probably his iPhone. Isabelle, check. The empty chairs seem to glare at him—the ghosts of Patrick and Bart—and Kevin thinks this makes sense. This toast is really for them.

"For years and years," Kevin says, "I felt like the Lesser Quinn. The slacker Quinn. The screwup Quinn. The unremarkable middle child. After all, I had an older brother who could slay dragons with his green eyes. I had a younger sister with perfect pitch. And just when it seemed my younger brother might end up being a bigger failure than even me, he goes off to war to defend our country and our freedom."

There is a sniffle from Mitzi's direction.

"But today I saw my little girl baptized, a daughter given to me by my beautiful fiancée, Isabelle Beaulieu. Some of what is good and right about my life is due to those of you who dealt with me before I met Isabelle—Mom, Dad, Mitzi, Jennifer, Ava, and my brothers, Patrick and Bart. But now, the love that sustains me and motivates me and keeps me upright is my love for Isabelle and for our precious, sweet daughter, Genevieve. It is to them that I would like to raise my glass. Thank you for saving me. Thank you for making me matter. Cheers to all, and God bless."

Cheers, God bless around the table. Even Jennifer raises her glass.

They order. Bisque for Drake, flatbread for Mitzi, lobster roll for Margaret, steak for Kelley, chicken fingers for Jaime, burger for Pierce, *nothing* for Barrett until he relents and orders the burger, bouillabaisse for Isabelle, grilled swordfish for Kevin, and a salad, no dressing, for Jennifer. Until she reconsiders and orders the fried shrimp platter with extra coleslaw.

Okay, Kevin thinks. They are on their way. Genevieve is asleep in Isabelle's arms and Isabelle doesn't look far behind. Kevin is so tired he could put his head down on the table now and sleep until morning.

The waiter leaves and Ava appears. She is not with Scott, as they all expected. She is by herself and her face is bright pink. She looks like a dam that's about to burst.

"Mitzi?" Ava says. "Daddy?"

Everyone at the table is staring at her.

Margaret seems to intuit what Ava is about to say. "Has something happened, darling?"

"I just heard on the radio that one of the missing marines from Bart's platoon has *escaped*. The U.S. military has him. He's in critical condition and is being flown to Landstuhl for treatment."

"What?" Mitzi says.

Margaret jumps up from the table with her phone.

KELLEY

He is the patriarch here. It's up to him to keep order and make decisions. They can't sit and enjoy lunch now; already their table sounds like a street riot.

Kevin asks the waiter to pack all the meals up to go and Jennifer says that she and the boys will wait for the food while everyone else heads back to the inn.

Mitzi is shaking so badly Kelley and Drake each take an arm and lead her out of the restaurant. She's saying, "One of the marines escaped. One escaped! That means the others are alive. Right, Kelley? Right?"

"We don't know," Kelley says. One marine out of forty-five escaped. What are the chances it was Bart? Three percent. And does Kelley *want* it to be Bart? The marine is in "critical condition."

But he's alive. And Mitzi's right. That means the others might be alive, too.

Hope.

Margaret is standing in the parking lot, phone to one ear, fingers plugging the other. Kelley and Drake walk Mitzi over to the car and help her inside.

Kelley wishes he'd eaten something. He does *not* feel

well. His head feels like it's going to topple off his shoulders.

Margaret finally hangs up and climbs into the backseat. She says, "They should be releasing the name within the hour."

Mitzi keens. Kelley gets behind the wheel. One thing at a time. He has to drive safely back to the inn.

Hope.

At home, everyone gathers in the kitchen except for Isabelle, who is putting the baby down for a nap. Jennifer comes in with heavy bags of takeout containers, which smell wonderful, although no one has any desire to eat.

Kelley pours himself a cup of coffee and sets about making some tea for Mitzi, which he knows she won't drink, but he wants to keep his hands busy.

They are all waiting for Margaret's phone to ring.

There's a knock at the front door. Ava looks at Kelley, who looks at Kevin. Kevin goes to answer it, and a few seconds later George walks into the kitchen. Kelley puts a protective hand on Mitzi's shoulder.

George says, "I just heard the news. I felt I should come."

Kelley nods and offers their former Santa Claus a stool at the counter. "Coffee?" Kelley asks.

George pulls out his flask. "Whiskey," he says.

"Good idea," Kevin says, and he pours himself a shot of Jameson. "Dad?"

"No thanks," Kelley says.

Jennifer takes a few Styrofoam containers out of the bag and says, "I'm going to take the boys up their lunch."

The second she leaves, there's another knock at the front door.

"Word is out," Kevin says. He goes to answer it. A few seconds later, Scott walks into the kitchen.

"I just heard," he says. He looks at Ava. "Are you okay?"

Ava shrugs.

"It's a waiting game," Drake says.

"Scott, can I get you a cup of coffee?" Kelley asks.

"I'm good, thanks, Mr. Quinn."

"We missed you at lunch," Kelley says.

"Yeah, well—"

Scott is interrupted by the ringing of Margaret's phone.

Everyone in the kitchen stops dead quiet, staring at the name on the lit screen.

Darcy.

The marine's name is William Burke. He is twenty years old, from Madison, Wisconsin. He is being treated for head trauma and various broken bones and lacerations. He was discovered by a civilian Afghani family. They took him to a U.S. military outpost on the outskirts of Sangin.

"That's all we have right now," Margaret says. "He's alive, he was strong enough to escape, and my source on the ground says officials are optimistic that most or all of the other soldiers are alive."

"Most?" Mitzi says.

"We just don't know," Margaret says. She hugs Mitzi tightly. "But this is *good* news, Mitzi. This is *good* news."

Tears drip down Mitzi's face. Margaret looks at Kelley and says, "We need this kid to live. If this kid lives, he can give the military valuable information."

"Valuable information," Kelley says.

"So that they can find Bart," Margaret says.

His son. His baby boy. Not a perfect kid by any stretch of the imagination, but a beloved child nonetheless. A child he and Mitzi had enjoyed and appreciated.

He hears Mitzi whispering under her breath. *Bart Bart Bart Bart Bart.*

It's Kelley who suggests they all go into Bart's room to pray. He and Mitzi, Margaret and Drake, Ava and Scott, Kevin, Isabelle, and Genevieve, Jennifer, the boys, and even George. They all file into Bart's room and, without words, join hands in a circle. The room smells like Bart was there five minutes ago—pot smoke, Doritos, dirty socks.

Kelley says, "Dear Lord, we are a family, prostrate before you, asking for the return of our son, our brother, our uncle, Bartholomew Quinn. Please bring him safely back to this island, back to this house, back to this family. And we pray for the recovery of Private William Burke and for his family and loved ones..."

Suddenly Kelley can't breathe. He can't get air in or out of his lungs. In his mind's eye is a picture of Bart's face in the seconds just after he got beaned with the baseball thrown by D-Day, who was a head taller than Bart, and three years older. He can see the pain on Bart's face and the urge to mask the pain, the desire to be brave, to shake it off, to stand back up at the plate and try to hit the ball again. *You didn't hurt me, you didn't scare me, pitch to me again!* This is the same attitude he will be exhibiting now, wherever he is. Bart grew up afraid of nothing because he never had any reason to be afraid. He, more than the older children, was certain of his talent, his charm, his good luck. He is alive somewhere and he is bravely plotting his own escape.

Kelley will see his son again.

It is the certainty of this that draws all of the oxygen out of Kelley's lungs.

"Amen," everyone says.

Kelley falls to his knees first, and then collapses on the floor.

"Kelley!" Mitzi screams.

Kevin and Ava simultaneously call 911. Drake kneels down to check Kelley's pulse. Kelley hears Drake say, "He's unconscious."

Bart, Kelley thinks. *This is good news,* he thinks.

Margaret says, "Help him, Drake. Help him!"

Mitzi says, "Kelley, baby, please wake up. Please, Kelley. Don't you leave me, too."

JENNIFER

Kelley is taken to Nantucket Cottage Hospital, where he will be kept overnight for observation and tests. It's exhaustion, the doctor thinks. Stress, low blood sugar. Nothing to be worried about, yet.

At four o'clock, after things have quieted down, Jennifer sits in an armchair in the living room, where she can see the twinkling lights and whimsical ornaments on the Christmas tree. She calls the prison in Shirley to talk to Patrick. The oxy has worn off and she resists taking another. She feels scooped out, and her nerves are frayed.

The one thing that never disappoints is how happy Patrick sounds to hear from her during their weekly phone calls. He sounds like he's been holding his breath for a week.

"Hey, beautiful," he says. "Do you know how much I miss you? Do you know how much I *love* you?"

"I do," she says. "And I miss you. And I love you."

"How was the weekend?" he asks. "Tell me everything."

Jennifer takes a deep breath. "Get ready," she says. "This might take a while."

AUTHOR'S NOTE

On the Friday of Christmas Stroll this past year, 2014, I lost a person whom I loved very much. Her name is Grace MacEachern and when she passed—suddenly, in her sleep—she was eight and a half years old.

Grace's parents, Matthew and Evelyn, are friends of mine. Evelyn is so dear to me she is more like family than friend. To an outside observer, then, it would seem that my friends lost their child, and like any parent, I keenly feel their loss and their unimaginable pain. However, I more than feel it; I share it. For I always felt that Grace was not just my friends' child, but my *friend*.

I am a novelist, but can I do a worthy job of describing Grace? I will try.

Grace was a life force. She was intense. She was brilliant and she had a huge, beautiful, room-brightening smile. Despite suffering a host of physical and medical challenges, the child never failed to *beam* and she never failed to ask a zillion questions in rapid succession. ("Hi, how are you? What did you eat for breakfast? What are you going to have for lunch? Do you have any lotion? Do you have any lipstick? Are you pregnant?") She learned my name at an early age, and when she caught a glimpse of me, she would come running and grab me around the legs. Her grip was ironclad. I like to flatter myself and think that I am really special and magnetic to children, but the truth was, Grace was super passionate about two things: Chapstick and cupcakes. I was good for one 100 percent of the time (Chapstick; I am never without it), and the other about 50 percent of the time (cupcakes; as we all know, I love to cook).

This past summer, when I was fighting breast cancer and going back and forth for my reconstruction appointments at Mass General, Evelyn and Grace would drop macarons from the Petticoat Row Bakery on my front porch. They were Grace's favorite and they are also my favorite, and Grace liked to get them for me because she knew I was sick and that I was busy getting better and that the macarons made me happy. Grace wanted everyone in her world to be happy and well. She had an uncanny sense of people, even adults, especially adults. Her kind and concerned manner, her empathy, belied her years.

Christmas Stroll is a magical time on Nantucket Island, and I will always love it. However, it will never be the same for me after losing my young friend. I loved her, she is gone, and I miss her. I marvel at the fortitude and the faith of her parents and her two brothers. For all of you readers who have children, I humbly ask you this: Please hug them a little harder tonight for Grace, kiss them one more time tonight for Grace.

Life is so, so precious.

Merry Christmas.

ABOUT THE AUTHOR

Elin Hilderbrand has spent Christmas Stroll weekend on Nantucket since 1998. She enjoys attending the annual Festival of Trees preview party at the Nantucket Whaling Museum and the Friends of Nantucket Public Schools Holiday House Tour. Her other favorite Winter Stroll traditions include making cheese fondue and decorating the tree with her three children. *Winter Stroll* is her sixteenth novel and the second book in the Winter Street trilogy.

. . . AND HER NEXT CHRISTMAS NOVEL

Gather under the mistletoe for one last round of caroling with the Quinn family in the heartwarming conclusion to Elin Hilderbrand's bestselling Winter Street trilogy. Following is an excerpt from the opening pages of *Winter Storms*.

MARGARET

Here is a little-known fact about Margaret Quinn: She likes some news stories better than others. At the bottom of her list are terrorist attacks, random shootings, and…the election. Margaret has to fight off her indifference on a daily basis. She has been on familiar terms with the past three presidents and her overwhelming emotion toward them wasn't awe or admiration, it was pity. Being president of the United States is the most stressful, thankless job in the world and Margaret can't fathom why anyone would voluntarily pursue it. End of topic.

Margaret's favorite kind of news story is—would anyone believe this?—the weather. The dull, the prosaic, the default I-have-nothing-else-to-talk-about-so-let's-talk-about-the-weather topic is, to Margaret's mind, a stunning daily phenomenon, overlooked and taken for granted. Margaret loves it all: hurricanes, tornadoes, blizzards, lightning storms, and—the ultimate bonanza—an earthquake followed by a tsunami. This may seem sadistic, but even as she mourns any loss of life, she is intrigued by the science of it. Weather is a physical manifestation of the earth's power. Margaret also likes that weather defies prediction. Meteorologists can get close, but there are no guarantees.

The world, Margaret thinks, is full of surprises.

*   *   *

Margaret's ex-husband, Kelley Quinn, has prostate cancer. He was diagnosed just before Christmas, which made for another muted, maudlin holiday. Margaret was tempted to take a leave of absence from the network in order to manage Kelley's care, but Kelley's estranged wife, Mitzi, returned to the fold and is now very much in charge. After twenty years of barely concealed animosity, Margaret and Mitzi have come to a place of peace, bordering on friendship, and Margaret would like to keep it that way—so she's backed off. She gets updates every day or two from her daughter, Ava. Kelley's cancer is contained; it hasn't metastasized. He has been traveling back and forth to the Cape five days a week for his radiation treatments. Mitzi goes with him most days, although she's made no secret of the fact that she finds the radiation aggressive. She would prefer Kelley to treat his cancer holistically with herbs, kale smoothies, massage, energy work, and sleep.

Margaret bites her tongue.

One thing that Margaret knows will make both Kelley and Mitzi feel better is getting definitive news about their son, Bart, who has been missing in Afghanistan since December of 2014. Margaret checks her computer first thing each morning for briefs from the DoD. One soldier from Bart's platoon, William Burke, escaped to safety, but he remains at Walter Reed in Bethesda. He sustained life-threatening head trauma and, hence, the DoD has no new intelligence about where the rest of the troops are, or even if they're alive.

But they might soon, Margaret guesses. Assuming the kid makes it.

The winter months are mild, a welcome change from the year before, and spring arrives right on time in the second half of March. It's not a false spring either, but a real, true spring, the kind portrayed in picture books—with bunny rabbits, budding trees, children on swing sets. Margaret's apartment overlooks Central Park and by the first of April, the park is a lush green carpet accented by bursts of color—beds of tulips, daffodils, hyacinths, iris. Model yachts skim across Conservatory Pond. There are soaking rain showers at night so that in the morning when Margaret steps out of her apartment building and into the waiting car sent by the service, the city looks shellacked and the air feels scrubbed clean.

It's a good spring. Kelley will be fine, Margaret tells herself. Their son Patrick is set to be released from jail on the first of June. He already has a handful of investors and he plans to open his own boutique investment firm. How he managed this from inside the lockup, Margaret isn't sure. She made him promise her that, from here on out, everything he does will be legal.

Margaret's granddaughter, Genevieve, is growing and changing each day. She can now sit up, and technology is so advanced that when Margaret and Kevin connect on Face-Time, Margaret can wave and coo and watch Genevieve laugh. Kevin and Isabelle are busy with the inn, which, thanks to the clement weather, has been filled to capacity since the middle of March.

But what is really painting Margaret's world pink is that she's in love. Dr. Drake Carroll has changed from a some-time lover to her constant companion, best friend, and fiancé. They'd both vowed to make time for the relationship to grow. Margaret had wondered if she would be able to keep her promise, and then she'd wondered if Drake would be able to keep *his*—but she has been pleasantly surprised at how organic and natural it is to be part of a couple again. Weeknights, they stay at Margaret's apartment, and week-ends, they're at Drake's. They go out to dinner downtown at places picked by Margaret's assistant, Darcy, who is a wizard at finding the most fun and delicious spots in the city—the Lion, Saxon and Parole, Jeffrey's Grocery, Uncle Boons. They've been to the theater three times, and they work out side by side at the gym; on Sundays, they order in Vietnamese food and watch old movies. Drake sends Margaret flowers at the studio; he writes *I love you* in soap on the bathroom mirror. Margaret is besotted. When you're in love, every day is like a present you get to open.

Margaret's daughter, Ava, wants to take a trip, just the two of them, before Margaret gets married. It will be a bachelorette trip to celebrate the end of Margaret's freedom! Ava says.

Margaret is lukewarm on the idea. The last thing she needs at her age is a bachelorette celebration. She harks back to a very drunken night nearly forty years earlier that found her roaming the West Village with her six bridesmaids. Alison, the leader of Margaret's bachelorette foray, had insisted they stop at a bar to hear acoustic guitar music and then further insisted that Margaret join the singer—a very cute guy with shoulder-length hair and a naughty gleam in his eye—onstage to sing "American Pie." Margaret impressed the crowd and the band so much with her voice and her knowledge of the lyrics that she got a standing ovation, and the lead singer asked if he could take her home.

No, Margaret had said. She had been genuinely confused. *I'm the one getting married.*

Obviously any trip with Ava would be a far cry from that, but at her age, even the word *bachelorette* makes Margaret cringe.

But one day, as she's kicking it up a notch on the treadmill, Margaret is struck by a realization. This trip Ava is suggesting isn't for Margaret—it's for Ava.

Her daughter needs her.

AVA

Using her mother's credit card and her mother's assistant, Darcy—who has an inexplicably deep reservoir of general knowledge, considering her young age—Ava books five nights in adjoining ocean-view suites at the Malliouhana resort in Anguilla over her spring break.

She needs to get off the island of Nantucket.

Her love life is in a state of emergency.

Through the winter and into the spring, she has been unable to choose between Nathaniel and Scott and so she dates them both. Has anyone on God's green planet ever successfully dated two men at once? Oh yeah? Well, how about on an island that is thirteen miles long and four miles wide? One night, when Ava was out with Scott at a romantic dinner at Company of the Cauldron, Nathaniel walked by outside, saw Ava, and started waving like a madman. He then proceeded to take a lengthy phone call right outside the window, directly in Ava's line of sight. Ava wanted Nathaniel to leave so she could finish her dinner with Scott in peace, but she also wanted to know who Nathaniel was on the phone with. He seemed to be laughing pretty hard. Another time, when Ava was with Nathaniel at Cisco Brewers having a Winter Shredder and listening to the Four Easy Payments, Scott walked in with Roxanne Oliveria, aka Mz. Ohhhhhh, who still had a slight limp from breaking her ankle in December.

Scott said, "Hi, Ava."

Roxanne said, "Oh, hello, Ava."

Ava sipped her Shredder and said nothing. Nathaniel raised a hand to Scott and said, "Hey there, Scotty boy," in a tone of voice that announced his victory. Roxanne smiled at Ava in a way that announced her victory, and then she requested "Brown-Eyed Girl," a choice Ava found over-played and obvious. Ava bumped knees with Nathaniel under the table, and although he certainly wanted to stay and make Scott uncomfortable, he asked for the check.

Ava has told Nathaniel and Scott that she is dating both of them, and she makes it clear they are free to date other people. Nathaniel says he has no interest in anyone but Ava. This is an effective strategy, especially since Ava has had trust issues with Nathaniel in the past and has, on occasion, questioned his devotion. On nights when Ava goes out with Scott, Nathaniel either stops in at the Bar with his crew or stays home and reads Harlan Coben novels; he always texts her when he's hitting the hay. When Ava is out with Nathaniel, Scott goes out with Roxanne. This is also an effective strategy. Ava suspected that Roxanne was making a play for Scott, but she'd never believed Scott would fall for it. When Ava is at school, she will sometimes see Roxanne emerging from the main office wearing one of her low-cut blouses and a tight pencil skirt and absurd wedge heels. Roxanne teaches English at the high school—two buildings away—and there is no reason why she should be at the elementary school except to lean over Scott's desk and let her long hair fall into her cleavage. Ava can't believe the superintendent hasn't spoken to Roxanne about the provocative way she dresses, and Ava can't believe Roxanne still insists on wearing heels even after she's broken her ankle on the cobblestones of Federal Street. Ava's real problem, however, is jealousy. She is insanely jealous of Roxanne. Roxanne is beautiful and alluring; the wedge heels make her calves look amazing. Roxanne has also, apparently, revealed her vulnerable side to Scott, something he is unable to resist. Roxanne has been through three broken engagements—Fiancé One was gay, Fiancé Two was a cheater, and Fiancé Three died in a surfing accident while on vacation in San Diego. Roxanne's loss of the third fiancé leaves

Ava unable to hate her. Scott confided to her that Roxanne still sees a therapist to cope with Gunner's death, and she bursts into tears over strange things—orange sunsets, the smell of lily of the valley, the song "Last Nite" by the Strokes.

Both Nathaniel and Scott have been available and supportive for Ava throughout Bart's continued absence and Kelley's illness. Nathaniel is better at *doing* things—he is the one who picks up Kelley and Mitzi from the boat or the airport after radiation; he is the one who wakes up early every day to check the DoD website to see if William Burke has made any medical progress or if any other troops from Bart's platoon have escaped. Scott is better at talking—he asks Ava how she feels about Kelley's illness (although outwardly optimistic, inwardly she's terrified); how she feels about Bart's disappearance (although outwardly optimistic, especially in front of Kelley and Mitzi, inwardly she's terrified).

Together, Nathaniel and Scott are the perfect partner. Ava would like to live with them both forever or be married to each of them on alternating weeks. But since that practice isn't acceptable in Western cultures, Ava will have to choose, and she can't choose.

She needs time away with the wisest woman she knows.

Are there any woes that a five-star hotel in the Caribbean can't fix? The Malliouhana resort is set amid lush, impeccably manicured gardens that are silent but for the sound of a gurgling waterfall and birdsong. The spa is down one winding brick path, the fitness center down another. The lobby is Moroccan inspired, with marble floors and rattan ceiling fans and gracious arches that frame the expansive view of the turquoise sea. Ava is further charmed by their connecting suites—pencil-post beds with crisp linens and piles of fluffy white pillows, enormous soaking tubs, French champagne in the minibar, and a bright-orange hammock chair on the balcony.

Who needs Nathaniel? Who needs Scott? Here, Ava has to decide only between her Jane Green novel and her Anita Shreve; between the hotel's infinity pool and one of three secluded beach coves; between rum punch and a glass of chilled rosé.

The first morning, Ava runs down the mile-long white crescent of sand that is Meads Bay, then, at the Viceroy hotel, she cuts in and runs another mile down the road. She passes a man, her age or a little older, who is wearing a Nantucket T-shirt and a hat from Cisco Brewers. Ava scowls—she can't get away! Nantucket is everywhere, even here on Anguilla! She gives the man a lame wave, then picks up her pace.

Margaret has gone to the fitness center and they meet for breakfast at ten o'clock in the open-air restaurant, both of them still in their workout clothes. At the buffet, Ava piles her plate with pineapple, papaya, and mango, whereas Margaret dives into the French cheeses, the ham, salami, and pâté, and the warm croissants. The woman can eat whatever she wants and never gain an ounce.

Ava sees the man in the Nantucket T-shirt sitting in the restaurant with a much-older gentleman, probably his father or his uncle or his boss. Margaret notices the Nantucket T-shirt and says to him, "Oh, my daughter lives on Nantucket!"

"No, Mom," Ava says, but it's too late, of course. The man whips off his hat and stands up.

He says, "You're Margaret Quinn."

Ava closes her eyes. She loves how her mother rolls through life like she's a normal person, seemingly unaware that every single soul in America—in the world, practically—recognizes her as the anchor of the *CBS Evening News.*

Margaret doesn't respond. Instead, she nudges Ava forward. "This is Ava," Margaret says. "She teaches music at the Nantucket Elementary School. Her father—my ex-husband—owns and operates the Winter Street Inn."

"Mom, he doesn't care," Ava says.

"No, I do care," the man says. "I'm Potter Lyons, and this is my grandfather, whose name is also Potter Lyons, but everyone calls him Gibby." Potter smiles at Ava. "I love Nantucket better than any place on earth. I go every August for Race Week. Do you sail?"

"We put her in sailing camp when she was seven years old," Margaret says. "There was a bully on her boat and she refused to go back. She hasn't sailed since." Margaret puts a thoughtful finger to her lips and turns to Ava. "Except that one summer when you sailed in the Opera House Cup."

Mom, he doesn't care! Ava thinks. He's only appearing interested because it's Margaret Quinn talking and she has a talent for making the mundane details of Ava's growing-up sound like national news.

Ava smiles at Potter and Gibby. "Confirmed," she says. "The bully's name was Alex, and in 2009, I sailed in the Opera House Cup on the *Shamrock*."

"They rent Sunfish here, down on the beach," Potter said. "It's not the *Shamrock*, but let me know if you want to go for a sail. I'd love to take you out."

Ava stares down at her plate of fruit. Her face is most likely the color of the papaya.

"Nice to meet you," she says. She leads her mother across the restaurant to the table farthest from Potter and Gibby.

"I think he likes you!" Margaret whispers.

No, Ava thinks. *He likes you.*

They bump into Potter and Gibby again at lunchtime at a place down the beach called Blanchards. Blanchards is a beach shack, and at first Ava is thrilled with the find. She and Margaret walk up to the counter in their bare feet and ask for one grilled mahimahi BLT with smoked-tomato tartar sauce, one order of shrimp tacos, and two sides of coleslaw. And while they're at it—two passion-fruit daiquiris.

Ava is so in love with the beach shack that she takes a picture of the menu and texts it to Kevin, saying, *You could do this at home! Quinns' on the Beach!* Kevin and Isabelle are running the inn, but Kevin has been looking for a second business opportunity. *This is it!* Ava thinks. Isabelle is a fantastic cook; she will be able to figure out the smoked-tomato tartar sauce, no problem.

Ava's reverie is interrupted by Potter and Gibby. "You've discovered our secret," Potter says. "We've eaten here six days straight."

"Jonum, phtzplz," Margaret says. Ava puts a hand on her mother's arm. The last thing Margaret needs is to be photographed with her mouth full of shrimp taco. She'll end up front and center in *Us Weekly*'s "Stars—They're Just Like Us!" (They talk with their mouths full!) Besides, Ava fears Margaret was trying to say *Join us, please.*

"We're almost done," Ava says, though she's taken only two bites of her heavenly sandwich.

"Hey, do you want to go for that sail later?" Potter asks.

Ava looks up at him. He's wearing orange board shorts and a white polo shirt. He has a little bit of gray in his dark hair, and his eyes seem very blue, probably thanks to his tan. He's way too handsome for her. He must be pursuing her because she's Margaret Quinn's daughter.

"Let me see how I feel later," she says.

The blue eyes light up. "Great!" he says.

When he and Gibby walk away, Margaret says, "You'd be a fool not to go."

"Mom," Ava says. "I have too many men in my life as it is."

"Sometimes what you need is a fresh perspective," Margaret says. "Go for a sail. It's not like you're marrying the guy."

Ava decides to ignore the fact that Potter is so good-looking and go for the sail. The first thing that happens is that the wind whips Potter's Cisco Brewers hat right off his head, and before either of them can react, it's dancing off toward the horizon.

"My favorite hat!" Potter says.

"Don't worry," Ava says. "I'll get you another one."

Potter Lyons is thirty-six years old. He's divorced and has a five-year-old son, also named Potter Lyons (though he goes by PJ), who lives with his mother in Palo Alto, California. Potter has a doctorate in American literature and teaches English at Columbia University. He wrote his dissertation on Jules Verne, *Twenty Thousand Leagues Under the Sea,* and he teaches the most popular class in the department, which is entitled the Nautical Novel: From the *Odyssey* to *Spartina.* He lives in a three-bedroom condo on the Upper West Side, only ten blocks north of Margaret, and he owns a sailboat, *Cassandra,* which he keeps at the New York Yacht Club.

"Was Cassandra your wife?" Ava asks.

"My grandmother," he says.

Potter then tells her that his parents were killed in a car accident when he was in high school, and his grandparents—Gibby and Cassandra—took over raising him.

"My grandmother died a few months ago," Potter says. "So I planned this trip for Gibby. He needed to get away."

"I'm so sorry," Ava says.

"But enough about me," Potter says with a grin. "What do *you* think of me?"

Ava laughs. She thinks he's charming and smart, and she loves that he brought his grandfather on vacation.

"Just kidding," he says. "I want to hear about Ava."